"Wake up, Sara, before you drown in your own delusions."

Lee's mouth curved brutally. "*Adjustments* is a play about repressed adolescent sexuality. You know it, and I know it. You simply won't accept it."

"I wrote *Adjustments*," Sara snapped, "and I *know* what it's about! You don't want to star in this play, you just want to ruin it. And as for delusions, the only one I had was thinking you and I could be friends!"

"Oh, no," he murmured, "we could never be friends. Passionate lovers or bitter enemies, but nothing so mundane as friends." His lean dark face came down and Sara shut her eyes, already aroused by his nearness. "It's for you to decide. Lovers or enemies. I don't want anything in between."

Books by Claire Harrison

CLAIRE HARRISON

leading man

Harlequin Books

TORONTO • NEW YORK • LONDON
AMSTERDAM • PARIS • SYDNEY • HAMBURG
STOCKHOLM • ATHENS • TOKYO • MILAN

Harlequin Presents first edition October 1984
ISBN 0-373-10727-7

Original hardcover edition published in 1984
by Mills & Boon Limited

CHAPTER ONE

SARA Morrison stood before the imposing façade of the Hotel Moravia and sighed as the wind whipped her shoulder-length hair around her face, each strand gleaming like copper wire in the cold afternoon sun. The sidewalk on Fifth Avenue was crowded with shoppers, their flow parting around her and then meeting again so that she stood like a small island, still and silent, isolated from their chatter and bustle. It was close to Christmas and there was a festive feeling in the air, an anticipation brought on by the decorations that hung on the light posts and the cornucopia of displays in the wide windows of department stores. Down the street from where she was standing, a Salvation Army Santa Claus rang his bell over a tripod that held a pot for charitable donations.

The jingle of his bell caught Sara's attention for a second and then she brought her mind back to the problem at hand, wondering if she dared leave and go home. It wouldn't cost her a job, but it would bring all the wrath of B.J. down on her head, and that was no easier to contemplate than the coming meeting. Sara grimaced, uncaring that she aroused the curiosity of passersby, and hitched her leather portfolio over her shoulder. She wasn't a coward, nor particularly shy, and there was no reason why her talk with Lee Cameron should go badly. All he wanted was information, and she was a walking encyclopaedia on his subject of interest.

Still, Sara thought as she finally pushed open the wide brass doors of the hotel, it wasn't going to be easy, and she mentally cursed B.J. for foisting the job on her, although it wasn't his fault that his brother had been taken ill in Miami. Nor was it his fault that Lee Cameron had arrived unexpectedly from Hollywood. But the two events had occurred simultaneously and B.J., caught between a family crisis and an important business deal, had been forced to make an awkward decision.

'You'll have to go meet Cameron.'

'Me?' Sara had stared at her employer in consternation.

'You,' B.J. growled emphatically.

'But I'm not the right person,' she had protested.

B.J. frowned at her, his blue eyes fierce. He was almost completely bald with only the slightest white fringe, but what hair he lacked on his head was made up for in his eyebrows. They were wide, bushy and white, and when B.J. was angry or annoyed or impatient, they drew together in a fiercesome, awe-inspiring bridge over his dominating nose. 'There's no one better,' he said.

'But you know how I feel about putting Lee Cameron in that part!'

B.J. chomped on his cigar. 'I know how you feel, but it doesn't change the fact that Cameron is here and wants to see someone from Banner Artistic Associates today.'

'And I suppose what Lee Cameron wants, Lee Cameron gets,' Sara said rebelliously.

Was there a twinkle of amused understanding in those blue eyes? If so, B.J. didn't give her any inkling of it. 'A man who can draw millions of dollars at the box office,' he said gruffly, 'can ask for the moon and all I'll need to know is if he wants it in slices or cubes.'

'But he's such a . . . a cowboy!' Sara cried.

B.J. had stood up from behind his massive mahogany desk with its three telephones, broad leather blotter and an in-basket piled high with the pleas and requests of hopefuls and looked down from his own impressive height into Sara's unhappy blue eyes. 'Cowboy or not, if Lee Cameron decides he wants the role of Dr Holme in *Adjustments*, I'm going to sign him. We'll get backers so fast that I'll have the play on Broadway in six months.'

Of course, B.J. was right; Sara knew that. He was an impresario in the old-fashioned sense of the word and handled big name bands, nightclub acts and the careers of some of the world's most famous actors and actresses. B.J. wheeled and dealed in the entertainment business and, in his small sphere of influence, he was a king.

But that didn't alter the fact that casting Lee Cameron in the part of the psychiatrist was a gross error of misjudgment; of that Sara was convinced. In each of his last three movies he had played a hired killer and the plots had involved the usual staple of murder, mayhem and macho action. Sara had seen his last one, *Danger Zone*, and vividly remembered his tough, dark looks and aura of raw sexuality. Why couldn't Lee Cameron stick to roles that suited him well? Why, she wondered dismally, was he interested in a role on Broadway that required a subtlety and finesse that was obviously far beyond his acting ability? Just the thought of Lee Cameron's virile swagger in the delicate role of Dr Holme made her want to cringe.

The softly lit lobby of the Hotel Moravia held an air of peace after the bustle of the sidewalk. It was the genteel and graceful quiet of old, established money. The patrons that walked past Sara were richly dressed and bejewelled, their faces smooth and well kept. The lights from multi-prismed chandeliers fell on the plush of thick burgundy carpets and discreet groupings of velvet chairs and sofas. There was no sound of the rushing traffic outside, and Sara had the sensation of being in another world, one that was far removed from

the ordinary, humdrum quality of normal life. She had
anticipated that Lee Cameron would travel in style, but
she hadn't thought he would choose the old elegance of
the Hotel Moravia. There were many newer hotels in
Manhattan that offered the latest in modern conveni-
ences; waterbeds, stereo decks and jacuzzis, and Sara
was surprised that a playboy of Lee Cameron's sort
didn't prefer their glossy glamour.

In the elevator to the penthouse suite, Sara took off
her coat and nervously twitched the straight skirt of her
suit even straighter. She looked exceedingly businesslike
in severe navy suit and matching court shoes, her outfit
only softened by the soft white lace jabot of her blouse
and the ruffles at her cuffs. The suit was quite adequate
for a meeting with a major movie star, but for a second
Sara had the very feminine wish that she had been
dressed in something more glamorous. She shook her
head and smiled ruefully. First of all, she quite detested
men like Lee Cameron, whose lifestyle was reputedly
decadent and whose reputation as a womaniser kept
gossip columnists in business, and secondly, she knew
that she didn't have a tinker's chance of making an
impression.

He was, no doubt, accustomed to starlets, ingénues
and the world's most glamorous women. She would
pass in and out of Lee Cameron's life like an
insignificant fly and wouldn't even be surprised if he
didn't notice her face. She was attractive by ordinary
standards, but not spectacular, and she'd had first-hand
acquaintance with the self-centred arrogance of celebrities. They were usually far too busy preening to
acknowledge the minions that floated in their orbit. It
would be too much to hope, she concluded, that Lee
Cameron would be any different.

The elevator stopped smoothly at the penthouse floor
and Sara stepped out into a quiet, carpeted corridor.
The double doors to Lee Cameron's suite were made of

carved oak, and just as she was approaching it, the brass handle moved and the doors swung open to reveal the undeniably curvaceous rear view of a woman who was wearing a black, well-cut dress and extremely high-heeled black sandals. Sara instinctively moved backwards against the wall but couldn't avoid overhearing the last bit of conversation between Lee Cameron and his guest.

'Darling, it's been lovely.'

'Any time, Regina.' The voice behind the door was deep and masculine with a timbre that had been known to send tremors through an entire female audience.

'I missed you, you know.'

'Was that before or after your latest conquest?'

Sara caught a glimpse of a delicate profile and a cascade of shimmering blonde hair. 'Lee! How can you be so callous? Philippe meant nothing to me.'

'And I do?' Did Sara detect a note of dry amusement?

'Of course.'

'Even though I lack a French accent?' Yes, there was definitely a sense of humour there, Sara thought.

'Darling,' the blonde purred softly, 'what does an accent matter in b . . .?'

Her last words were stifled as a pair of lean, dark hands pulled her forward. Sara squirmed uncomfortably all through the pause that followed. It was one thing to know in the abstract that Lee Cameron had a horde of girl-friends, but it was quite another to face it in the flesh or hear the sounds of it coming through the door. It was with relief that she saw the blonde back out again, a small smug smile on her lips as she passed Sara, her mascaraed green eyes sweeping over the navy suit with indifference and disdain. In the brief second that their eyes met, Sara recognised a leading model whose face had adorned every fashion magazine in the country. One could either credit Lee Cameron with impeccable taste, Sara thought as she turned to watch Regina walk towards the elevator, or castigate him for overlooking brains in favour of beautiful packaging.

'Yes?'

Sara turned back to find a pair of dark eyes surveying her from the centre parting of her red hair, over the slender oval of her face and along the trim line of her suit to the tips of her plain brown shoes. She had the uncomfortable feeling that they missed nothing and had noted the fact that she was taller than average, that her hair waved naturally, that a spray of minute freckles lay across her nose and that her legs, easily her best feature, were long, slender and had a delicately turned ankle. 'Sara Morrison from Banner Artistic Associates,' she said, clearing her throat.

Even darker eyebrows pulled together in a frown that could rival B.J.'s in ferocity. 'I was expecting Mr Banner.'

Sara's smile wavered. 'He was unable to come. His ... brother in Miami went into hospital unexpectedly.'

'I see,' Lee Cameron said slowly. 'Well, come on in.'

Sara followed him into the suite, shocked to find that her knees were trembling slightly. The star of *Danger Zone* was unexpectedly formidable, his face far more striking in person than it had ever been on the screen. It wasn't a handsome face, but it was one that held an odd combination of savagery and sensuality, particularly in the incisive curve of the mouth. His hair was black, tousled and damp as if he had just come out of a shower, and he wore a pair of hip-hugging black jeans and a white silk shirt that opened at the neck revealing a tanned, muscular throat. His screen presence had also minimised the lithe grace in his six-foot frame and the total impact of his virility. Sara had never been immune to masculine charms, but she'd never been overwhelmed either. It was a new experience to find that her pulse rate could increase merely by being in the vicinity of a exceedingly attractive male.

'Sit down, Miss Morrison,' he invited.

'Thank you.'

'Would you like a drink?'

Sara shook her head, a little too quickly. 'No, thank you.'

Lee Cameron glanced at the way she sat on the edge of the chair, her hands demurely clasped together. One eyebrow lifted. 'You don't mind if I have one?' he asked.

Sara was startled. 'Of . . . course not,' she stammered.

As he walked over to a mahogany buffet table that held a tray of bottles and glasses, Sara glanced at the suite, noting the rich blue of the curtains, the plush white carpet and the bottle of champagne in a sterling silver cooler. A copy of the play, *Adjustments*, lay on the coffee table before her, and it had been read so many times that its edges were dog-eared and the cover ripped off. She reached for a book that had been carelessly tossed beside it and found, to her surprise, that she was holding Shakespeare. Light reading matter for Mr Cameron? she wondered. It was hard to believe that the star of *Danger Zone* had anything more on his mind than the right brand of whisky, the pistol he packed and the speed of his last car chase.

'Do you like Shakespeare, Miss Morrison?'

Sara looked up from her perusal of *Love's Labour's Lost* to find that Lee Cameron had come back and was standing close to her. She shifted uneasily horrified to discover that her mouth had suddenly gone dry and her palms were slightly damp. Nervously, she set the book back in its place.

'I read him occasionally.'

He sat down in the chair next to the couch and sipped at his tumbler of Scotch. 'But you're surprised that I do?'

Sara didn't like the feeling she had that he could read her mind. 'No, of course not.'

He changed the subject abruptly. 'You're Mr Banner's assistant?'

'Yes.'

'Are you competent to talk about the play?'

Sara refrained from smiling. 'I think so.'

Lee Cameron leaned back in the chair, his shoulders broad against its curved edge, and stared at her for a second, his dark gaze unreadable. 'You're sure you won't have a drink, Miss Morrison?'

'No, thank you.'

'You don't drink?'

Sara unconsciously tugged at her skirt hem, making sure that it covered her knees. 'Not when I'm on business.'

'Would you like a cigarette?' He gestured at the pack on the coffee table. She shook her head. 'No, thanks. I don't smoke.'

His lips moved into a slight, unamused curve. 'Sex?' he asked bluntly.

'I . . . beg your pardon!'

Lee gazed mockingly at the flush on her cheeks and the widened blue of her eyes. 'Relax,' he said, 'I was just wondering if you indulged in any of the ordinary human vices.'

Sara gave him a cold smile. 'We seem to have got off on the wrong foot, Mr Cameron. I'm quite human.'

'You've been giving off an air of righteous priggishness since you appeared in the doorway.'

'I wasn't expecting to find you . . .' Sara sought for the right word.

'Entertaining a woman?' he suggested.

'Yes,' she said defiantly.

'Perhaps the circumstances are not what they appear.'

'Really, Mr Cameron, what you do is your business.'

The lamp light caused his hair to gleam blue-black. 'You disapprove of me, Miss Morrison, don't you?'

Sara fervently wished that she could turn the clock back half an hour and start all over again. It was true that she disapproved of Lee Cameron. She didn't like the movies he played in or his reputed playboy lifestyle, but she hadn't expected that he'd be perceptive enough to notice.

'Mr Banner said that you wanted to discuss *Adjustments*,' she said firmly.

Lee Cameron acknowledged her tactic with a derisive nod of his head. 'I'm interested in the part of the psychiatrist. It's a very complex role.'

Sara frowned. 'I would have called it straightforward,' she said.

'Straightforward? On the contrary, I would call Dr Holme Machiavellian.'

She stared at him. 'Machiavellian?' she echoed incredulously.

'You don't think so?'

'I think the psychiatrist is concerned about the young girl, Maria. He wants to cure her and allow her to be a normal person.'

'Have you actually read this play?' He was looking at her in disbelief.

'Of course,' she said.

'Then why haven't you noticed the way he manipulates Maria and her mother?'

'He doesn't manipulate them,' she protested. 'He's trying to help them.'

'You don't think that the psychiatrist is setting himself up as a sexual idol? That he intends to entrap both the mother and daughter into a type of sensual adoration?'

Sara gave him a horrified look. 'That's ridiculous!' she said vehemently.

He put his glass of Scotch down on the table so hard that the pale golden liquid splashed over the edge. 'Why the hell did Banner send you here anyway?' he demanded angrily. 'You don't even have the vaguest idea what this play is about!'

'That's not true,' Sara retorted between clenched teeth.

He reached over, picked up his battered copy of *Adjustments* and opened to a page. '*"Your daughter is quite vulnerable,"*' he quoted, his voice low. '*"She both hates you and wishes to be like you, Mrs Evans, but we know, don't we, that no thirteen-year old can ever be like her mother."*' He looked away from the script towards Sara. 'What would you call that?'

Sara took a deep breath. 'He's trying to comfort the mother; he's trying to explain why Maria has stopped talking.'

'And you don't hear any hint of the man's overriding sensuality?'

'Don't you think of anything besides sex?' Sara flared at him.

His dark gaze was mocking. 'I think, Miss Morrison, that you would deny the role of sex in this play.' And he flicked the pages of the script as if every word in it was subject to his interpretation.

Sara's back was rigid, no longer touching the couch at all. 'It's the story of a girl's realisation that she's not responsible for her parents' actions and mistakes.'

'Is it?' Lee Cameron asked silkily.

'Yes,' she said curtly.

'And you don't believe that it has anything to do with her understanding that she's on the verge of being a woman?'

Sara shook her head vehemently. 'No.'

'Interesting, isn't it, that you and I should come up with such a difference of opinion.'

'You can think what you like,' Sara responded with a shrug.

His lip curled. 'As long as I don't play the part of Dr Holme?'

Sara wasn't accustomed to sabotage, but Lee was

handing her the opportunity to destroy B.J.'s efforts in one fell swoop. The temptation was overwhelming and Sara could justify it with an assortment of facts. If Lee Cameron didn't want the role, there were several other well-known stage actors who would possibly jump at the chance of playing Dr Holme. And she was sure that Lee Cameron wasn't the only actor who could draw financial backing. Sara had seen B.J.'s long list of potential money sources and suspected that he'd be able to find the capital somewhere. B.J., she knew from experience, could cajole money from even the most miserly.

She stared defiantly into his dark eyes. 'Yes.'

Instead of being angry, he seemed to find her negative appraisal amusing. 'You're a strange woman, Miss Morrison. My impression of Banner Associates was that they'd bend over backwards to get my signature on a contract.'

'Mr Banner would like you to sign,' Sara agreed reluctantly.

'So you're not actually representing Banner Associates.'

'I have my own opinions.'

Lee Cameron had put down the script and picked up his glass of Scotch again. Now he turned it slowly in his hands and stared into the depths of the amber liquid. Sara found herself unable to look away from the steady movements of his lean fingers or the firm muscularity of his wrists. His hands were not effete or soft; they looked as if they were accustomed to work, to handling things, to touching . . . things. She forced her eyes away and looked down at the velvet texture of the couch and the way the strands of gold weaved in among the blue.

'Why did you come here, Miss Morrison?'

The voice was soft but its command was not. Sara was forced to meet his eyes. 'Mr Banner was unable to . . .'

'Why did you come here?'

She swallowed and discovered that her mouth was dry. 'To discuss the play.'

The line of his mouth was hard. 'And convince me that I shouldn't take the part?'

Sara sought the courage to confront him. 'I don't think you're right for the role.'

His voice was cold. 'Why?'

'You're far better at . . . at movies like *Danger Zone* where . . .'

'I'm not a novice, Miss Morrison, and I'm not afraid of criticism. Why don't you think I suit the role?'

She bit her lip. 'Well, you're too young, for one thing.'

He gave her an incredulous look. 'Too young?'

'Dr Holme is a part for an older man – someone in his fifties.'

'A fatherly type?'

'Yes,' Sara said in relief, pleased that he had understood.

'Doesn't it strike you as peculiar that the mother, a sophisticated woman in her thirties, would be attracted to a man, a fatherly sort of man, easily twenty years older than herself?'

Sara had a sudden feeling of faintness. 'The mother isn't attracted to the psychiatrist.'

Lee Cameron leaned forward and stared at her intently, one lean, high cheekbone turned to bronze by the lamp. 'You don't think so?'

Sara had difficulty speaking. 'No.'

'What else is wrong with me?' he asked softly.

She didn't know where to look. His dark eyes probed at her as if they sought to unravel the thoughts that twisted in her mind. 'It's . . . your image.'

'Too sexy?'

'Too . . . too macho.'

'You don't like men who are macho?'

She avoided the question. 'Dr Holme isn't macho.'

'What makes you think that I couldn't play a stage role that is different from my movie roles?'

She looked away from him. 'I've never seen you do anything else.'

A muscle leaped in his jaw. 'Aren't you condemning me prematurely, Miss Morrison?'

Was she? Sara contemplated her entwined fingers and wondered if Lee Cameron wasn't right. The similarity of his movie roles didn't necessarily mean that he couldn't be radically different in something else, and she knew that even before meeting him she'd been prejudiced about his acting ability. Still, Lee Cameron was so far, physically and temperamentally, from the Dr Holme she envisioned that she simply couldn't accept him.

'Perhaps I am,' she said slowly, 'but I'm afraid that you're not Dr Holme.'

His expression was unreadable and Sara, glancing at him surreptitiously through her lashes, thought how pagan he appeared; dark and sinister. No wonder he'd been chosen to play a killer so many times, his face suited the role with its hard planes and arrogant jut of nose and jaw. And even though he sat immobile, she could feel the coiled tension in his muscles and sensed the watchfulness that lay behind his seemingly relaxed pose. ·

'Why,' he asked at last, 'are you taking such a personal interest in this play, Miss Morrison?'

It was the question she had dreaded, and Sara took evasive action. 'I'm interested in all the plays that Banner Artistic Associates handles.'

'Are you?'

She could see that Lee was not fooled. 'Yes.'

'Are you a personal friend of the playwright?'

Sara took a quick glance at the script that lay in his lap, confirming what she had noticed earlier – that the cover with the name of the playwright was missing. 'Positive,' she said with emphasis, staring directly into his eyes.

If he was taken aback by her assurance, he showed no indication of retreating. Instead he moved immediately into an attack. 'I'm sorry,' he said, leaning even further back in the chair, lazy elegance in every line of his body, 'that our interpretations of the play are so different, but I've decided to take the part of Dr Holme anyway.'

Sara felt a sudden heat rise to her face, the slow burn of her anger causing a tightness to press against her chest. 'In that case . . .' she said, standing quickly to her feet, 'then I suppose that we have nothing more to talk about.'

'No, I don't think we do.'

The derision in his voice made tears come unexpectedly to her eyes and she turned so that he couldn't see her face. Blinded, she banged against the coffee table in her urgency to leave and, in a second, Lee Cameron was standing next to her, his hand firmly at her elbow.

'Can I help you?' he murmured.

'No!' Sara attempted to pull her arm out of his grasp and only succeeded in losing her balance against the couch.

He steadied her and then his lean hand cupped her chin, forcing her face upwards. She blinked at him, her dark lashes damp and spiky, and inwardly cursed the tears that showed how vulnerable she was to the mocking slant of his mouth.

'Really, Miss Morrison, is this necessary?' His thumb gently wiped a tear off her cheek.

'I'd like to leave. Please let me go.'

He ignored her. 'All this emotion for a play?'

Sara wrenched her chin from his hand. 'I cry over grocery lists, too,' she said curtly.

'Could it be, Miss Morrison, that it's the wrong time of the month?'

Her eyes widened in shock that he would mention something so intimate and then, in fury and outrage, she reached up and slapped his face, her palm hard and flat against the lean plane of his cheek. The sound of it seemed to ring in the silence of the suite, echoing and reverberating against the walls.

He pinioned her wrist in a tight grip, and they stared at one another for a long minute while the imprint of her hand on his face reddened into an angry flush. 'I think,' he said, his eyes narrowed, 'that you'd better tell me what's at the bottom of all this.'

'Nothing.'

'I don't believe you,' he growled.

Sara swallowed. 'I can't stop you from playing Dr Holme.'

'Why the hell do you care so much?'

'I . . . like the play. It's good. I don't want it ruined.'

'To the point of coming here and putting your own ego on the line? Come on, Miss Morrison, I'm not so stupid. Have you put your own money into the play? Your life savings?'

Her copper hair swayed on her shoulders as she shook her head. 'No.'

Lee Cameron tightened his grasp of her wrist. 'Then why?' he demanded, and Sara realised that he wouldn't let her go until he knew the truth.

'It's a personal matter,' she stammered.

Triumph gave a deep glint to his eyes and he dropped her wrist. 'You and the playwright *are* friends.'

'No,' she whispered.

'Relatives?'

'No.'

'Lovers?'

Denial was written across her face, and Lee Cameron took a sudden step backwards when understanding hit him. 'I don't believe it,' he said slowly, glancing over at the script on the chair and realising that he had never even known the name of the playwright since the cover had disappeared weeks ago. 'I don't believe it.'

'It's true,' she said in a low voice, 'I wrote it.'

'How the hell could you have written that play and still be so ignorant about what's in it?'

Sara was stung. 'It's *you* that doesn't understand!'

He crossed his arms across his broad chest and leaned back slightly upon his heels, his eyes mocking. 'I'm still going to take the part.'

She looked at him in shock. 'But . . . you can't!'

'I can do as I please,' he said.

'But I wrote the play, I know the kind of actor who should take Dr Holme's part.' She could hear the pleading in her voice, but couldn't stop herself from begging. How could he insist on denying her interpretation now that he knew she was the playwright? She had a terrible urge to slap him again, to shake the arrogance out of him, anything that would force him to admit that he was making a mistake.

Lee Cameron merely looked amused. 'Sometimes the author is the last to know.'

'The last to know what?'

'What he or she has created.'

Sara pressed her hands together. 'Believe me,' she said with great intensity, 'I know what I've created.'

'It's quite obvious that you don't have a clue that you've written a play about a sexual triangle.'

Her heart pounded with such force that Sara could hear it in her ears. 'It isn't a sexual triangle at all—it's just a simple story about a girl who's deeply unhappy about her parents' divorce and needs to be cured.'

He shook his head in irritated disbelief. 'That may have been what you originally intended, but the result is quite different.'

'It can't be different!'

'You've put words in the mouths of your characters that are full of sexual innuendo.'

Sara bit her lip in desperation. 'You're reading far too much into it. I . . . I know those characters so well. I know what's happening in that play.'

He was unconvinced. 'You can't see the forest for the trees.'

'But don't you see? I know Maria; I . . .' Her voice faltered and he suddenly gave her a quick, appraising look.

'Yes?' he asked.

The words trembled on her lips, hovering tentatively in space. She had never told anyone, not even B.J. Would it change Lee Cameron's mind if he knew her secret? Could she convince him that he shouldn't take the role of Dr Holme? Could she trust him? For a second, Sara stared at him and knew that he was unlike the man she had anticipated meeting. He was far more perceptive and more intelligent than she had imagined. Perhaps he'd be understanding; perhaps he would acknowledge the truth when he heard it.

'Why do you know Maria, Miss Morrison?' he persisted, his voice low and soft.

Sara shivered, not knowing if it was the husky timbre of his voice that played upon her nerve endings or the realisation that she was going to speak a truth that had been deeply buried into the past. 'I know her,' she began hesitantly, 'because . . . because I was Maria.'

CHAPTER TWO

WHEN Sara let herself into her apartment, she could smell the scent of spaghetti sauce cooking and knew that her cousin, Elissa, had skipped her afternoon college classes.

'It's about time you got home,' Elissa called from the kitchen, and then her face appeared in the doorway. 'What kept you?'

'Business.'

Elissa wiped her hands on her apron. 'Is B.J. acting like a slave driver again?'

Sara's mouth twisted in a wry smile. 'Did he ever stop?'

Her cousin ducked back into the kitchen with a grin and a wave, while Sara hung up her coat and then sank down into the couch, leaning her head against its back and closing her eyes in exhaustion. The apartment always comforted her; she had designed it with serenity in mind. The floor was carpeted in a smooth grey and the furniture, plain in design, was upholstered in a mute blue. She had painted the walls a soft white and covered the windows with white shades. The only counterpoints to the almost Oriental simplicity of the room were the lush green plants that stood on a glass-topped table. Sara lazily reached out and touched the long leaf of an abundant spider plant, caressing its cool smoothness with her fingers, imagining its deep green behind the dark barrier of her eyelids.

'You really are beat, aren't you?'

Sara opened her eyes and found Elissa standing before her, a frown of concern on her freckled face. They had both inherited the Morrison copper-red hair

22

and blue eyes, but Elissa had managed to capture most of the freckles in the family. They dotted her nose, her plump cheeks, her square chin and even her ears. 'In my next life,' she had told Sara one morning as they shared the bathroom mirror, 'I'm going to ask for a cream and rose complexion, hair the colour of a raven's wing and a figure like yours.'

'What's wrong with yours?' Sara asked.

'What's wrong with it?' echoed Elissa with a wail. 'It's short, square and stocky, a deadly combination that turns men off immediately.'

Sara had shaken her head reprovingly. 'I think you have a cute figure,' she had protested.

Elissa had turned back to the mirror, twisted her face into a gargoyle's grimace and shook her short copper curls. 'What's cute when I could be tall, svelte and glamorous.'

'I'm not glamorous,' Sara had protested with a laugh.

Her cousin eyed her, obviously slender and curvaceous despite the enclosing folds of her flannel nightgown. 'Well, you're a lot closer than I'm ever going to get,' she sighed enviously.

Sara had merely smiled, surprised again at how much she had come to like Elissa. They were first cousins and had grown up in the same suburb of New York, but they had never been close. Sara was four years older and had spent most of her adolescence trying to ignore Elissa and her younger brothers' mischievous behaviour. By the time she had moved to Manhattan and settled down into a job and an apartment, she'd forgotten all about her cousin except for the occasional memory of a chunky little tomboy with a pair of unkempt red braids and a tendency towards sloppy clothes. Letters from her mother kept her informed of family comings and goings, and Sara had noticed without any particular interest Elissa's awards as a cellist, her graduation from high school and acceptance into the Juilliard School of

Music. What Sara hadn't expected was the pressure the family put on her to share her New York apartment with her cousin, their reasons ranging from financial considerations to her own presumed loneliness at living by herself.

Sara had resisted, argued and then conceded, mainly because of her Aunt Betty, Elissa's mother. She couldn't forget the kindness and love her aunt had given her during the period of her parents' divorce and reasoned that the least she could do to repay that devotion was put up with Elissa. To her astonishment, however, the arrangement had worked out well. Elissa was no longer a rough tomboy with a taste for embarrassing practical jokes. She'd matured, was responsible and neat, and had developed a sense of humour that kept Sara from taking life too seriously. The four-year separation in their ages no longer seemed very important. Their friendship, Sara now thought as she gave Elissa a wan smile, went beyond such trivial differences.

'Would a little bit of chilled red wine revive you?' Elissa asked.

Sara sat up. 'Wine? Since when do we have wine?'

'Ah,' said Elissa mysteriously. 'A little genie decided to treat us to a bottle of wine to share with our spaghetti and salad.'

Sara made a knowing grimace. 'Little, my eye,' she retorted.

Elissa grinned. 'Okay, not so little.'

'Peter invited himself again?'

'Not exactly, although he hinted broadly that he was starving and required sustenance, preferably prepared in our kitchen.'

Sara sighed. 'Couldn't you have put him off?'

Her cousin waved a scolding finger in the air. 'Shame on you, cousin! Have you no feelings for your fellow man?'

Sara groaned and got up from the couch. 'I'd better get changed, it's going to be a long evening.'

She went into her bedroom and tried to concentrate on thinking about Peter Gray. It was one way of keeping her mind off Lee Cameron, although it wasn't entirely successful. She would have liked to blank out the memory of her interview with him, but parts of it kept replaying in her mind like some lousy Grade B film: her prim façade, his macho illusions to sex and that horrible slap in the face. God, she'd acted like some overwrought heroine in a melodrama! And, of course, it had got her nowhere. Lee, at the end, had promised her nothing except another reading of the play. He hadn't probed into her background or asked her to explain anything, and Sara had been forced to leave without having gained a thing and with the excruciating feeling that she had suffered a severe loss of dignity and self-respect.

She was far too much of a realist to entertain any hope that Lee would give up the idea of playing Dr Holme. He was the kind of man who seized opportunities when they came and pursued them with single-minded diligence. She could only pray that he might view the character of Dr Holme in another light now that he knew that the play had been written from her own personal experiences. His interpretation of the role with its sexual overtones had deeply offended and shocked her. Her memory of the real Dr Holme was of a genial man who wore tweedy jackets with leather patches on the elbows and smoked a pipe. He had been gentle, kind and sympathetic, and the relationship between them had been nothing more than that of doctor and patient. There had never been a hint of seduction; after all, she had only been thirteen at the time. Sara pursed her lips and could not resist speculating that Lee Cameron must have had some rather peculiar experiences in his own past to warrant such nasty suspicions.

With that satisfying thought, she hung her suit away in the closet and pulled on a pair of jeans and a blue turtleneck sweater and then brushed her hair, clipping it back against her temples with tortoiseshell combs. She stared into the mirror for a second, noted the paleness of her complexion and decided against anything more elaborate than a bit of lipstick and blusher. Peter had seen her in every imaginable form of sloppy attire and probably never even noticed that she tended to dress down in his company rather than dress up. He was that sort of man.

They'd met over a broken water fountain on Riverside Park Drive, a few blocks away from Sara's apartment building. It had been summer and she had been jogging for half an hour, finally quitting when the combination of heat and humidity made her wilt. She had stopped for a drink, bent her head over the fountain and been sprayed by a sudden and unexpected geyser of water. When she'd come up for air, spittering and sputtering, her face and hair drenched, the front of her T-shirt soaked to the skin, Sara had found a large man with shaggy brown hair and a lazy smile watching her. The ensuing conversation, lighthearted and flirtatious, had led to a shared pizza, an evening at the movies, several concerts and a one-sided, lopsided love affair that sometimes made Sara feel desperate.

There was no doubt that Peter adored her. He was thirty, six years older than she, and divorced. He was also large, amiable and cuddly, attributes that led Elissa to describe him as a teddy-bear. Sara couldn't help liking Peter; he was easy on the nerves and didn't seem to mind when she broke dates and was busy with her writing or her job. And he was downright handy. Peter was always there when you needed him—to fix a tap, pick up a gift or run to the nearby deli for bread or milk. Somehow, with absolutely no encouragement on her part, Peter had become a permanent fixture in her life. He played the benevolent uncle to Elissa and ardent devotee to Sara, and there were times when she could wring his neck in pure frustration with his smiling, agreeable presence.

Now why couldn't she be attracted to Peter the way she was to Lee Cameron? The thought made Sara's eyes widen and she gazed deep into the black depths of her own enlarged pupils, her mirrored reflection showing comical surprise. She couldn't deny that she had found Lee attractive in an overtly masculine way, but then he was a man whose sensuality was second nature, who knew how to flaunt his virility before a camera for the express purpose of seducing the imaginations of millions of women. Her attraction towards him was purely a chemical thing, not born of any emotional entanglement. Sara could think of nothing more disastrous than taking someone like Lee seriously. He had women throwing themselves at his feet, their hearts and bodies eager to flavour his particular sample of manhood. Sara gave a rueful smile and acknowledged to herself that Peter's less than dynamic personality offered a measure of safety with an appeal all of its own.

Still, Sara couldn't help contrasting the two men later when she sat in the living room and watched Peter fill his pipe and light it. He was slow and deliberate in all his actions; Sara had never known him to make an opinion without giving it grave thought beforehand. She guessed that he was probably very good at his profession. Peter was in banking and she could imagine his careful handling of money, the slow weighing of choices and the cautious investments. He inspired trust. His features were homely but not unpleasant, the kind of face you grew used to and then discovered that you liked more than you would have thought possible.

Sara could not imagine Lee Cameron sitting opposite her, drawing slowly on a pipe and calmly waiting for it to catch. His vibrancy could not be hidden, even his silences were merely a thin mask for his coiled energy. Lee had the intensity of a predatory animal and the unpredictability of the wildest creature. No woman could sit in his presence and know exactly what he would say next as Sara sat there waiting for Peter to remark, as he always did, about how much he liked her living room.

The pipe lit and Peter sighed with satisfaction. 'It's so nice and peaceful in here,' he said, then noticed Sara's expression. 'I guess I've said that before.'

'The trouble is,' Sara remarked, 'that you haven't bothered to decorate your own place.'

Peter shrugged his big shoulders. 'It's just a room, it doesn't seem like home.'

'Why didn't you find something bigger? You could have afforded it.'

'I just needed a hole to crawl in after the divorce.'

She glanced at him sharply, wondering if she detected a note of bitterness in his voice. Peter rarely talked about his ex-wife or the circumstances around his separation and divorce, and Sara had respected his silence, considering it the height of bad taste to be nosy about someone else's problems. But now for the first time, she had a desire to find out what lay beneath his phlegmatic exterior. Was he really so easy-going, or was he hiding something? A core of anger? A river of discontent?

'Was it so awful?' she asked sympathetically.

Peter glanced up from his pipe. 'The divorce?'

Sara nodded.

'Pretty bad, I guess.'

'What was she like?'

'Karen?' he paused for a long thought. 'A pretty woman with a lot of flair for certain kinds of things.

She was a mixer, she liked to entertain and have friends around her. Every night I came home, she'd be having someone to dinner.'

'And you didn't like that?'

'I didn't mind, but I wasn't good at it the way she was. It made her angry—she had a quick temper.'

Sara couldn't help but feel a certain pity for the unknown Karen. Opposites were known to attract, but in this case, the marriage must have been a disaster. Peter could never be a social butterfly. He was not particularly good at small talk and he preferred peace to chatter. It was one of his attributes that Sara liked; there were often silences between them, comfortable ones when Sara could think about other things; her job, a dress that she wanted to buy, her next writing project.

'Anyway,' Peter continued, 'she decided that I didn't want to live the same lifestyle she did, so we broke up. She met someone else right after that or maybe she was already seeing him. I never really figured that one out.' His brown eyes looked bewildered and hurt, and Sara unaccountably was reminded of a puppy she'd had as a child that never understood why it was being reprimanded or scolded. 'She kept the apartment and the furniture, she'd chosen it all and I didn't like it that much anyway. I took our investments. We both worked and we'd both paid for the stuff, so I guess it was fair. She wanted me out pretty fast and I took the first place I could find. I didn't think that I'd still be there three years later, but that's how it goes.'

Not the most articulate explanation of a divorce that Sara had ever heard, but it was a fair amount coming from Peter. She could read a bit between the lines and guessed that there was a lot about his former wife that Peter wasn't saying. She obviously hadn't enjoyed the very solid comforts that he had offered her and had, perhaps, traded the excitement of an affair for the security of her marriage. Sara wondered if they had fought a lot, although she couldn't imagine Peter engaging in any sort of verbal fracas. It was far more likely that Karen with her quick temper had hurled one abuse after another into his heavy silences and then given up in sheer frustration.

'The two of you look like an old married couple ready for a retirement home,' Elissa commented, walking into the living room and standing there with her hands on her hips.

Peter gave her a grin. 'Go do your homework, kid,' he said in a mock-patronising tone.

Elissa flung herself down on to the rocking chair and stretched out her blue-jeaned legs. 'I'm taking a night off.'

'I'm going to call the school,' he threatened. 'They'll cut you off the honours list.'

'The old fingers are tired,' she said, wiggling them in the air. 'I'm giving the cello a well-deserved rest.'

'Gaborsky giving you a hard time?' asked Sara. One of the things she admired most about Elissa was her dedication to music, but she had come to recognise the signs that her cousin and her teacher had just come through an unpleasant confrontation.

Elissa's mouth twisted downwards. 'If Gaborsky was burning in hell, I wouldn't even notify the fire department. If he was waiting to be executed, I'd make sure the guns were loaded.' She paused for a second, then added with fiendish relish, 'No, a hanging would be preferable. I'd open the trapdoor myself.'

Peter shook his head in amusement. 'He really got under your skin today, didn't he?'

It was no secret that Elissa's teacher, mentor and inspiration had a personality that could sour milk. He was an internationally acclaimed cellist and Elissa, whose dream it was to achieve the same heights, had to put up with his temper tantrums and overwrought artistic sensibility for the privilege of his instruction. Sara, who had heard about him long before meeting him, had been surprised to find that Gaborsky was a tiny, inauspicious little man with a small white moustache and a few strands of hair combed across a bald scalp. If it hadn't been for Elissa's tales, Sara would have assumed that he was the meekest man on earth.

'Let's talk about something else,' Elissa sighed.

'You want to hear about the latest interest rate?' asked Peter.

'God forbid!' Elissa groaned. 'If you don't watch it, I'll have you listed in Ripley's as the world's most boring man!'

Peter took his pipe out of his mouth. 'I might consider that a compliment,' he said challengingly.

Elissa rolled her eyes dramatically towards the ceiling. 'You would!'

As Sara watched them settle down to a game of chess, it occurred to her that Elissa brought something out in Peter, a latent wit and sense of humour, that no one else could. Elissa poked and prodded at him, never giving him a chance to fall back into his customary quiet and phlegmatic state. He, in turn, found her highly amusing and played straight man to her comedienne routines, a situation they both enjoyed immensely.

Sara opened a mystery novel that she was reading, but found that she couldn't concentrate on its complicated plot. The big question in her life was what to do about Peter. Half a dozen times a day she considered telling him the truth about her feelings and the other half a dozen she felt guilty and ashamed. How many of her friends wished they had a constant, reliable escort who gave them a daily dose of tender, loving care? And she liked Peter, she really did. If they married, she would have a comfortable life, free from financial and emotional hassles. A lot of women married for less than that.

Still, Sara was well aware that something vital was missing, although she knew that she would never be able to convince Peter. Whenever she did try to talk about their relationship, he would assure her that liking often deepened into love and that their personalities matched well. He thought she merely needed time, but Sara wasn't sure it wouldn't take a *life*time. Peter didn't excite her, he didn't make her nerves tingle with anticipation or her heart quicken one beat from its normal place. Lee Cameron had had that effect, she remembered with an unconscious shiver, then squashed the thought quickly. It was unfair to compare Peter to Lee. Unfair and hopeless.

B.J. arrived back in Manhattan over the weekend and was already deep into a pile of papers when Sara arrived in the office early on Monday morning. She peered into his doorway, saw him furiously scratching away at a paper and then tried to tiptoe away.

'I saw you,' he called accusingly, 'and I want to talk to you.'

Sara marched back into his office, gave him a snappy salute and sat down in the leather chair opposite his desk. 'How was your brother?' she asked.

'He's going to live.'

'And your sister-in-law?'

'Batty as ever,' he said curtly. 'Why my brother married that woman I'll never know.'

Sara kept her smile to herself. B.J., being a bachelor, didn't believe in marriage at all. It was an institution, he maintained, that had been developed by the devil for the sole purpose of plaguing mankind. He scorned every statistic which proved that married men were the happiest, sanest and least likely to be sick or commit suicide. 'Gerrymandered by married men,' he had grumbled when Sara had once shown him an article on the sad state of bachelors. 'Misery loves company, don't

you know that yet?' But Sara was privately inclined to
the view that B.J., for all his bluff and rumble, was
basically afraid of women. Whenever one of his
actresses went into a temper tantrum or indulged in
tears, B.J. would be out of his office faster than a
speeding bullet, giving Sara the high sign to get in there
and do *something*.

Sara loved working for Banner Artistic Associates. It
had been her first and only job in New York. She had
started out as the receptionist, a coveted position that
came through a friend of a friend. Eager actresses, she
had known, would have given their right arms to work in
the office of an impresario. Later, she had learned that
B.J. steered clear of any employee who had even the
slightest ambition to being on the stage. Would-be
starlets became flustered when a director showed up or
a famous actor or a well-known playwright. 'Mushes
their brains,' B.J. had told her. 'They think they're
auditioning when they're supposed to be taking
shorthand.'

Sara had passed the stage-struck test and had proven
to be unflappable on the phone, a tremendous asset in
dealing with hysterical actors, irate directors, nervous
backers and weaselly agents. She had been promoted to
secretary and then to B.J.'s personal assistant. The
office was always busy and the pace hectic. Sara thrived
on the commotion, the bustle and the constant
sensation that horrible disaster or fantastic success
hovered around the corner. She'd seen deals fixed and
deals broken, watched actors agonising over their
careers and handled sums of money so large that their
totals were almost beyond her comprehension.

And she enjoyed working for a man who was one of
the best in the business. When she had finished her
play, the culmination of years of scribbling short stories
and poems into notebooks, Sara had never thought of
giving it to anyone else other than B.J. After weeks of

trepidation and with the absolute conviction that he'd return it with a few kind words and not much enthusiasm, Sara had submitted the script to him. To her surprise, he had been immediately interested, had had her rewrite several sections and then begun the arduous process of bringing it to the stage. So far, Sara had agreed with everything he had done. Only Lee Cameron had proven to be a bone of contention.

Looking at B.J. now, Sara put off the moment of truth. 'You've got a bit of a tan, B.J.,' she remarked conversationally, noting the pink tinge of his bald head. 'Enjoy the Miami sun?'

'You know I hate being out in the sun,' he growled.

'Really, B.J.? You never mentioned that.' Sara gave him a wide-eyed look of innocence.

He glanced at her sharply, his blue eyes bright and suspicious under the bushy ledge of his eyebrows, taking in the severe coil of red hair on her neck and the very businesslike cut of her grey dress. 'A report, please, on your meeting with Lee Cameron.'

Sara cleared her throat nervously. She had known that B.J. would want to hear what happened with Lee Cameron, and she knew that she was going to have to shade the truth, not the easiest task under the gimlet eye of B.J. but a necessary one. She couldn't imagine giving him an unexpurgated version of the meeting. She would soften it a bit, leave out the sexual parts, her own revelation and, she hoped, convince him that Lee's indecision had nothing to do with her.

'Let's see,' she said, pulling a notebook out of her bag and consulting a scribbled page. 'We met at seven at the Hotel Moravia at the penthouse suite. Mr Cameron was, upon my arrival, entertaining Regina Delahunt, a well-known model and playgirl.'

'Playgirl?' One of those formidable eyebrows slanted forty-five degrees.

'As opposed to playboy,' Sara explained with a straight face.

B.J. harrumphed. 'Keep going.'

'She left and I went into the suite. It was very nice, B.J., and very expensive. The carpet was . . .'

'Sara!'

Well, so much for the camouflage and diversionary tactics, Sara thought ruefully. 'Mr Cameron and I discussed the play for approximately half an hour. He was exceedingly interested in the part of Dr Holme; he called it,' she glanced at her notebook, '"very complex".'

B.J. took a cigar out of the box on his desk and leaned back in his wide leather chair. 'Well, I'm glad to hear that he doesn't think it's going to be a piece of cake. His agent told me that he's eager for a Broadway role, but he's got to understand that it'll be more demanding than the movies.'

'Do you think he could act the role?'

B.J. gave her an intent look. 'What do you think? It's your play.'

Sara frowned. She would have liked to insist that Lee had no talent at all and would be a disaster in *Adjustments*, but that wouldn't be the truth. Meeting him in person had dispelled her opinion that he was all brawn and no brains. Although she still didn't want him to play the role of Dr Holme, she had the feeling that he really could act.

'I think he could do it,' she said reluctantly.

'Good. Go on.'

'Mr Cameron was still uncertain whether he wanted the part at the end of our meeting and said he would go over the play again before deciding.'

'You couldn't sell him on the idea?'

'B.J., you know I didn't want to *sell* him on the idea in the first place!' Sara protested. 'I still think he's the wrong man.'

'Even after meeting him?'

'More than ever.' She leaned forward intently, her hands gripping her notepad so tightly that the knuckles were white against her skin. 'He means to alter the entire theme of the play. He seems to have the crazy idea that Dr Holme is some kind of ... Machiavellian monster.'

B.J. lit his cigar, his blue eyes half covered by their lids as the smoke swirled around his head. 'You don't say.'

Sara played her trump card. 'He thinks that the psychiatrist is out to seduce both Maria and her mother.'

Instead of appearing shocked, B.J. lazily watched a smoke ring waft its way towards the ceiling. 'And you don't?'

'Of course not,' Sara declared.

B.J. put his cigar down and eyed her flushed face. 'You wrote that play from your own experience, didn't you?'

She was appalled that he had guessed the truth. 'I ...'

B.J. waved his hand in a negative motion. 'No need for confessions. I'm not interested in any sordid details from your past.'

Sara got control of herself. 'I know what I wrote, B.J., and Mr Cameron does not.'

'You aren't the first playwright who's sat in that chair and complained, Sara. Writing a play isn't the end of a process; it's the beginning. The director will change it, the actors will bring it to life. You can't alter its development simply because you were its author.'

She had known this and would never have guessed that the process would be so painful when applied to her own play, but she was still convinced that Lee's interpretation went far beyond the actual scope of *Adjustments*. 'Lee Cameron is trying to translate his own sexy image from the screen on to the stage,' she protested.

'Did you find him sexy?'

B.J. spoke with words casually, but Sara felt the implication behind them and she flushed. 'I can't deny,' she said slowly, choosing her words with care, 'that he is a very attractive man.'

'And you don't think Dr Holme is an attractive man?'

'His personal appearance isn't important to the plot of the play!'

He swung his chair around closer to her. 'Let me put it differently. Was the man you based the psychiatrist on attractive?'

'He was ... B.J., I don't see how this pertains...'

'Why are you trying so hard to eliminate the role of sex in your play?'

Sara gaped at him. She had never imagined that B.J. would be siding with Lee. Did all men have only sex on the brain? 'The play is about misunderstanding and family relations and...' Her voice trailed away under his fierce blue stare.

'Face it, honey,' he said curtly. 'This play is about sex, too. You may not have meant to put it there, but it's lurking between the lines.'

'But nothing happens!' Sara protested.

'That's because Maria is in every scene. Naturally the psychiatrist and the mother aren't going to make love in front of her.'

Sara felt the blood rush to her face as her heart pounded in heavy beats, but she tried to hide her reaction. 'Are we finished?' she asked, the cool tone of her voice belied by its hesitancy.

If B.J. knew what she was feeling, he didn't show it. He reached for a file folder and scowled. 'Nothing more to report?'

Wordlessly, she shook her head.

'Do you want me to continue?'

'Continue what?'

'You can pull the play, Sara, and it will never see the light of day.'

She stared into his wide, florid face and saw that he understood her dilemma. If she let the play go on, she might never be happy with its production. If she stopped the play from going on stage, all that she had worked for would be worthless. She thought of the time and effort that had gone into writing *Adjustments*; years of thinking, long nights of work and an entire summer holiday spent at her desk. She had been driven to write that play in a way different from any of her other literary ambitions. Some of it had seemed to spill out of her, coming from a deep part of her subconscious; other parts had required difficult and painful sessions of writing, rewriting and rewriting again.

All along the way, the dream of seeing it come alive had kept her going. She would never have called herself particularly greedy for success, but on the subject of this play, she had found she was different. She so badly wanted it on Broadway where thousands of theatregoers would see *her* play, *her* drama, *her* creation. And the characters were so alive, so vibrant, that the thought of consigning them now to oblivion made her feel physically sick.

'No,' she said slowly. 'I want it to go on.'

B.J. gave her a quick look and then said without any particular inflection, 'Good. Then I think this will be of interest to you. I found it under the door this morning when I let myself in.'

He handed her an envelope with the words, Banner Artistic Associates, written on the front in a clean decisive script. She opened it slowly, knowing even before she read the message inside what it would say. 'It's from Lee Cameron, isn't it?' she asked, unwrapping the creamy vellum paper in her shaking fingers.

'Yes.'

The note was short, clear and precisely to the point.

Have decided to take the part of Dr Holme. My agent will be in contact with you this week. Signed, *Lee Cameron*.

'You knew all along!' Sara breathed.

B.J. didn't look the slighest bit recalcitrant. 'I thought I'd give you a chance to tell your side of the story and make the choice.' He opened the folder in front of him, and Sara could tell that his mind was already on the next piece of business.

She stared at the top of his bald head and knew exactly why B.J. was one of the best impresarios in the business. He had played her very shrewdly, giving her the bait and all the rope that she needed to commit herself. She had made her objections to Lee Cameron, but without actually knowing that he would be in the play, she had also come to a decision about its survival. By pulling her up so short, confronting her with the choice of killing the play, B.J. had made her see just how she valued *Adjustments*. Sara knew that she wasn't going to allow one actor or one interpretation to keep the play from being staged.

'I don't have to like it, though,' she said in a low voice.

B.J. glanced up, his eyebrows in two white arcs of surprise as if he hadn't expected that she'd still be standing there. 'Never said you did, honey, but that's showbiz!'

CHAPTER THREE

ONCE Lee had made his decision to play the leading man in *Adjustments*, Sara was caught up in a whirlwind of activity even beyond the normally hectic pace of the office. The producer and director for the play were hired and there was a continuous set of conferences about staging, costumes, rehearsal schedules, theatre bookings and auditions. As B.J. had predicted, when the notice of Lee's casting was written up in *Variety*, money flowed in, a rich stream of cash that promised to make her play the most well-funded of the year. Sara, who kept the books and took the phone calls, was astonished at the number and type of people who wanted to join the bandwagon. She sometimes wondered how Lee would feel, knowing that the hopes and dreams of so many people rode on his reputation. To her, it seemed like an awesome responsibility.

In January the auditions began for the two actresses who would play the roles of the mother, Donna Evans, and the daughter, Maria. Sara was too busy at work to be able to attend the first round, but when the number of aspiring actresses was narrowed down and those chosen called back for a second try, both she and B.J. were there.

They sat in one of the middle rows of the darkened theatre and watched the actresses go through their paces. Since the cast was so small, only three people, the choice seemed infinitely more difficult than if a musical were being staged, and the actresses were asked to read several long scenes. The one that caught Sara's eye for the role of the mother was a well-known Broadway actress, Constance Donegal. Although she wasn't beautiful, she had an arresting face with wide dark eyes that were extremely expressive. She immediately caught the central feature of Donna Evans' character, a veneer of sophistication underlain by deep insecurity.

B.J. was also taken with her. 'She's the one,' he whispered to Sara as they watched Constance pace the stage, reading from the script.

'I think so, too,' she whispered back. 'You think David and John agree?'

He waved his hand at the director and producer who sat several rows in front of them. 'They know quality when they see it.'

The part of Maria was more difficult. It called for an actress who could look thirteen and was excellent at mime. Maria never left the stage during the play, but also never said a word, except for one exclamation at the end of the play. For two acts and four scenes, she was required, by the use of facial expression and body language, to express a wide range of emotions; fear, unhappiness, rejection, anger, love and acceptance. To Sara's surprise, the actress who surpassed all the others being auditioned was an unknown.

Her name was Felicia Stevens and she was quite extraordinary. Although she was twenty-five, she was tiny and had the boyish shape of a young girl, an image reinforced by the pixie cut of her blonde hair and a snub nose beneath round green eyes. The director had her mime several different kinds of actions and emotions, and she seemed capable of twisting her body into contortions and her face into expressions that were incredibly vivid. When she was asked to be unhappy, every inch of her body drooped with sadness, every line of her face was etched with depression.

When John Hart, the director, asked her where she had gained her acting experience, Felicia said that she had come from a circus family. 'We were the clowns,' she said into the darkness of the almost empty theatre, and then immediately became a clown, walking around the floor flat-footed, thumbs stuck into an imaginary set of suspenders, her wide mouth in the permanently upturned grin of a buffoon.

John laughed, conferred with David Small, the producer, and then, turning in his seat towards B.J., made a signal with his hand which B.J. returned. John turned back to the stage. 'It's yours, sweetheart,' he called up to the stage.

Felicia suddenly stopped clowning. 'Mine?' she asked hesitantly.

'If you want the part.'

'You ... mean I get to play Maria?' The voice was breathless.

'Yup. Rehearsals start next week.'

Felicia stood for a second frozen to the ground and then, as if the news had suddenly hit home, gave a tiny, awkward bow and said, 'Thank you.' She looked beyond the director to where Sara and B.J. were sitting and bowed to their shadowy figures. 'Thank you,' she called out. And then, in a gesture of fierce exultation, she threw her arms out wide to encompass the whole of the theatre. 'Thank you!' she yelled and, to Sara's astonishment, the voice that came from that tiny body seemed to shake the very rafters of the building.

'That girl was terrific,' B.J. growled into his cigar as Felicia ran off the stage. 'I think I'll sign her before any other agent gets hold of her.'

'She's ... very good,' Sara agreed.

B.J. noted her hesitation. 'You didn't like her?'

Sara couldn't put her feeling into words. Felicia had been wonderful, and she suspected that they had just witnessed the beginning of a great star's career, but she somehow didn't like the idea of the actress as Maria. 'Shes's not vulnerable enough,' she said at last.

'I'm not sure any actress would please you, Sara.'

Sara glanced quickly at this heavy profile. 'Why?' she asked.

'You're too close to it, baby. Way too close.'

B.J. was probably right, she reflected. How could she choose an actress to play herself? No one could exactly fill the position with every characteristic of that long-gone but very well-remembered thirteen-year-old. Still, there was something about Felicia Stevens that struck Sara as wrong, although she couldn't put her finger on it. 'I don't know,' she said.

'Trust my instincts,' said B.J. 'The critics are going to fall all over themselves in superlatives.'

She shrugged and sighed. 'Do I have a choice?' she asked.

He laughed, then patted her hand in an avuncular fashion. 'It'll be all right,' he said. 'Don't worry about it.'

Sara wished she could have followed B.J.'s advice, but it was easier said than done. As the staging of the play gathered momentum, worry became her constant companion. It didn't help to know that she no longer had any control or power over *Adjustments*, she worried anyway, even to the point of dreaming about it. Her nights were disturbed with dark, twisted images of Lee and Felicia, Lee and Constance. She dreamed that they argued, fought and then embraced in blatantly sexual positions. She began waking up in the morning to discover that her sheets were tangled and damp and that her head ached even before she sat up. Finally, in the desperate hope that she could get a decent night's sleep, she asked B.J. if she could be spared from working on *Adjustments*.

He looked up from a sheaf of papers on his desk and frowned at her. 'Who will do it?' he growled.

'Stephanie could,' she said, mentioning one of the secretaries who was quick, smart and efficient.

B.J. leaned back in his chair, his massive shoulders dwarfing even its wide leather back. 'Why?'

'I can't handle it. You were right, I'm too close.'

'Hmmmph.' He gave her a disgruntled look, then asked, 'Is that why you haven't gone to a rehearsal yet?'

Rehearsals had started a week before, and although Sara had an open invitation from the director, she was reluctant to go. She didn't know what she was afraid of finding, but something held her back. She hadn't guessed, though, that anyone would notice her absence. 'Apologise to John for me,' she said, 'but I just don't want to watch.'

B.J. contemplated the dark circles under her blue eyes and the drawn look around her mouth and gave another harrumph. 'All right, I'll let Stephanie take over the details.' The telephone buzzed and Sara reached to pick up the receiver when he stopped her by placing his hand in her way. 'It isn't John who needs the apologies,' he grumbled.

Her eyes widened in surprise. 'Oh, I thought . . .'

'It's Lee. He's been wondering why you weren't there,' B.J. concluded drily, taking his hand away from the telephone so she could answer the call.

Funny, she thought later as she sat at her desk, that Lee should have been the one to remark on her absence. She would have thought that he had barely given her a moment's thought after she had left that night. As far as she knew he had gone back to Hollywood to finish a movie the day after their meeting and then flown back to New York the day before rehearsals began. Even if Sara hadn't worked for Banner Associates she would have known of Lee's arrival in Manhattan. It was broadcast in the gossip columns of every city newspaper and tabloid. From them, she learned that Lee had rented a luxurious suite on the upper West Side, that he had hired away a well-known politician's personal chef, that he had favoured a famous department store by buying a new suit there and that Bell Cleaners on West End Avenue had been chosen to clean his clothes. 'It's an honour,' Mr Bell had told the newspaper reporters with a wide grin, 'to help Lee Cameron be a success in our city.'

Sara, finally disgusted with reading about the intimate details of Lee's life, had turned back to the news section with a relief, thankful for the impersonality of crisis, famine and political intrigue. Now, she wondered how Lee stood the publicity that revealed every nook and cranny of his life to the predatory eyes of the curious. He wasn't the sort of man who thrived on his celebrity status, she had sensed that. He was a man who thrived on challenges. Why, otherwise, would he have staked his career on *Adjustments*?

'Why?' a deep voice said as if its owner could read her thoughts, and Sara looked up to see Lee standing in the doorway of her office.

'Why?' she echoed blankly, trying to suppress the sudden quickening of her pulse at the sight of him. He was lounging against the door sill's wooden edge, one hand in the pocket of his dark slacks, his black leather jacket unzipped to reveal a white turtleneck sweater stretched across the taut width of his abdomen and chest. Snow had been falling all day and some flakes, half-melted, dampened the thick strands of his hair, making the ends curl slightly. From the buzzing sounds behind him, Sara guessed that his entrance into the office had sent the typing pool into a frenzy.

'Why haven't you come to a rehearsal?'

Sara ignored his question and stood up. 'Come in,' she said, 'and please shut the door behind you.'

Lee, giving a wry, knowing glance into the room behind him, stepped forward, pulling the door closed with his hand so that the sound from the outer office was silenced, and they stood facing one another. Sara discovered that she had not in the least forgotten Lee's look of arrogance; the taut line of his jaw, the harsh aquilinity of his nose and the sensual curve of his mouth. No wonder the sighs of the girls in the typing pool could be heard above their typewriters! Lee embodied every woman's fantasy of male virility.

He looked away from her and glanced around at her office, noting the neat piles of paper on her desk, the almost spartan furnishings and the watercolour on one wall. He strode over to it and examined the small painting. It was a picture of the ocean done by an American artist, known for his vibrant use of colour.

'Very nice,' Lee commented. 'I didn't know you were a collector.'

Sara sat down at her desk, nervously smoothing the pleats in her cream silk dress. She didn't like to admit it, but her knees were weak. 'I'm not. It was a gift from B.J.'

'I see.' Lee walked back to her desk and sat down on it, one booted foot swinging. 'Do you usually accept gifts from your boss?' he asked, looking down at her.

Sara's glance was cold. 'When I deserve it,' she snapped. 'And no sexual suggestions, please. I've worked for B.J. for years.'

He threw up his hands in mock surrender. 'Sorry. I forgot how touchy you were on certain controversial subjects.'

'Touchy?' She glared at him. 'Don't you think that I have a right to be insulted when you immediately assume that my boss, who is also a good friend, only gives me gifts when . . . when . . .'

Lee supplied her with the words she didn't want to say. 'When you sleep with him?' he asked in amusement.

She drew herself up. 'This is not Hollywood, Mr Cameron, or the movies. I've heard about California.'

'Ah, yes—the state of sin. We positively wallow in it. And the name is Lee.'

For a second Sara thought he was serious, but his dark eyes held glints of laughter, and she couldn't restrain her own smile. 'All right . . . Lee,' she conceded. 'It's a bit of an exaggeration.'

'We Californians are used to prejudice. It comes with the territory.'

'Actually,' she confessed, 'I've never been there.'

'Not much of a traveller?'

'Rents are very expensive in New York,' she replied.

'You mean you can't even afford a taxi to Broadway and 59th Street?'

Sara gave him a rueful look. 'I don't want to see the rehearsals,' she admitted. 'I don't even want to think about the play any more.'

Lee's dark eyes held a sudden understanding. 'It frightens you.'

'Yes.'

'You might be able to give us some input.'

She shook her head. 'No.'

'It's going very well, you know,' he said gently. 'There's nothing to worry about.'

Sara only answered the first part of his statement. 'B.J. says it's going to be a smash.'

'Constance and Felicia are marvellous.'

She dipped her head in acknowledgement. 'I saw their auditions.'

The phone rang and Sara answered, thankful for the interruption, although still aware that his eyes were resting on her bent head and the thick coil of her red hair. His watchful gaze made her feel uncomfortable, as if the impeccable tailoring of her dress had come unravelled or her make-up had suddenly disappeared, leaving her unprotected and vulnerable. And there was an undeniable tension in the air. They had both, so far, been careful to avoid any mention of the role of Dr Holme or the disagreement that existed between them, and that very avoidance gave an undercurrent to the conversation that was disturbing.

The telephone call, involving a complex transaction of funds and payroll, was longer than Sara had expected, and when it was concluded, she turned to apologise to Lee but found that he had moved to the chair beside her desk and leaned back, his eyes closed. For a second, she had a free and unhindered view of his face. There were shadows under his eyes, deep lines around his mouth and nose, and he seemed much paler than she remembered. Dissipation or exhaustion, she thought, then chided herself for even considering the former. For all she knew, Lee had his nose to the grindstone. Sara was well aware how hard actors worked during rehearsals, and he would be working harder than most. His reputation rode on his success or failure for the two hours of opening night.

'Finished?' he asked, opening his eyes.

Sara blushed. 'Sorry. It's a famous face.'

'Too famous,' he said drily.

'I've been reading about you in the newspapers.'

'Do you know the brand of underwear I buy?' he asked.

'Not yet,' Sara said with a smile.

Lee ran a lean hand over his eyes in a gesture of fatigue. 'Read the *Enquirer* tomorrow. They'll probably tell you.'

'They asked!?'

'I think they bribed the salesman at Brook's Brothers.'

Sara shook her head in bemusement. 'Have you thought of disguising yourself?'

'It's crossed my mind,' he admitted, 'but I still cling to the illusion that I'm a free man.'

His tone of irony touched her. 'Don't give up,' she said softly.

Lee leaned forward and took one of her hands. 'Join

me for dinner tonight and help me fight off the adoring throng.'

'I . . .' The warmth of his hard palm and the way his thumb stroked her wrist made her falter.

'I need a bodyguard,' he said with a teasing smile.

Sara had been exposed to the hard side of Lee Cameron and borne the brunt of his anger and frustration, but she'd never known that his charm could be quite so devastating. 'All right,' she said, then shaking herself out of the spell of his soft voice and gentle caress, added reprovingly, 'but no more California-type insults.'

'Cross my heart,' said Lee, standing up. 'I'll pick you up at eight.'

By seven-thirty, Sara was dressed, perfumed, ready to go and in a state of agitation. It wasn't until after Lee had gone that she began to wonder why he was taking her out in the first place. To talk about business? Was he going to wine her and dine her elegantly in the hopes of getting her to agree to his interpretation of Dr Holme? Or was he really interested in pumping her about the past?

Sara had no intention of feeding Lee with details about the triangle of characters in the play and how they related to her own life. He was, she believed, quite capable of twisting everything she said to fit his own theories. One of the reasons she didn't want to go to the rehearsals was that she couldn't bear to watch Lee turn Dr Holme into a twisted sexual maniac. Her only hope lay in John Hart's ability as a director. She'd had a meeting with him about *Adjustments*, but it wasn't until John had gone that Sara had realised how one-sided their conversation had been. She had talked and John had listened, only occasionally asking her a question and making a comment. Sara had thought he was sympathetic to her viewpoint, but she now was no longer sure that he was in agreement.

The idea that Lee was taking her out to dinner for the mere plesasure of her company never really crossed her mind, since she had long ago brushed aside any idea that Lee could be interested in her as a woman. The competition was far too fierce for that and she wouldn't have been at all surprised if he had several women on the string at once. Regina Delahunt on the east coast, she thought as she checked her watch for the umpteenth time, a nubile startlet on the west coast, and heaven knows what in between.

The fact, however, that Sara had decided that the dinner date was not an attempt at seduction hadn't stopped her from an agonising debate over her wardrobe. She'd tried on every dinner dress she owned and had changed her hairstyle three times. She finally chose a low-cut black dress with narrow straps that criss-crossed her bare back and had a flowing silk skirt. She piled her copper hair on her head and skilfully applied enough make-up to make her blue eyes seem wider, tone down the spray of freckles on her nose and emphasise her cheekbones. By the time she had clasped on her grandmother's sapphire necklace around her slender neck and stepped into a pair of high-heeled silver sandals, Sara had come to the conclusion that she might not be model material but she'd done the best job with the materials available.

'Imagine, a date with Lee Cameron!' Elissa sighed as Sara paced the living room floor, trying to think of all the ways she could fend off Lee's inquisition probing into her life.

'Not a date,' Sara corrected her instantly. 'A business meeting.'

Elissa switched gears smoothly. 'Imagine a business meeting with Lee Cameron that takes places in an elegant restaurant and requires a low-cut black dress and the Morrison sapphires!'

'You're sounding adolescent,' Sara said accusingly.

'It's a phase I never grew out of,' her cousin confessed. 'I'm forever stuck in dreams of being kissed by a tall, dark and handsome man, falling in love at first sight and being swept off my feet—not necessarily in that order.'

'I don't believe in love at first sight.'

'Sara, the only thing I get to hug on a daily basis is my cello. Allow me a few dreams.'

Sara stopped her pacing to look at Elissa in surprise. Her cousin always seemed so busy and so nonchalant about men that it had never occurred to her that she was lonely or unhappy. 'Isn't there anyone at school?'

Elissa's wide mouth turned down. 'We're all such dedicated musicians.' She shrugged. 'Maybe if I lost twenty pounds and let my hair grow . . .'

Sara sat down on the couch beside her. 'You're not overweight and I think your hair is cute the way it is.' She tugged at one of Elissa's bright copper curls. 'Don't worry—the right man will turn up.'

Elissa, who could never be serious for long, batted her eyelashes at Sara. 'Maybe Lee has a friend?'

Sara fell in with her mood. 'But you have such stringent qualifications, Miss Morrison. If I recall properly, you were mentioning that the gentleman must be tall?' She mimed opening a notebook and readying a pen.

'Not a speck under six foot.'

'Dark?'

'And suave.'

'Handsome, I believe?'

'Sexy will do for starters.' Elissa suddenly gave Sara an odd look. 'What about Peter?'

Sara checked the imaginary notebook. 'Peter isn't dark or . . .'

'I mean about tonight. He's going to be jealous when he finds out.'

Sara shook her head impatiently. 'There's nothing to be jealous about. It's business.'

Elissa looked knowing. 'Can't business be discussed in the office?'

Sara shrugged off the uneasy feeling that the other girl's words engendered. 'Lee wants to talk about his part in the play. He probably considers it more civilised over dinner than next door to the typing pool.'

'What's with you and Peter lately? He's been very morose.'

Sara stood up again and walked to the window of her apartment, which looked out over the Hudson River, its water dark and rippled under the moonlit sky. It was a cold, clear night. Overhead, the stars were visible, their tiny points competing with the colourful glitter of the Manhattan skyline. Below her, a ribbon of cars wound along a freeway, an endless stream of traffic that continued all day and through most of the night. Sara had sometimes wondered where all those people were going and what their lives were like: so many strangers, each bound up in their own loves, hates and desires.

'Peter is far more serious about me than I am about him,' she said at last.

'He's a lot more sensitive than you think,' said Elissa in a serious tone. 'He talks to me about you sometimes.'

Sara threw out her hands in a helpless gesture. 'I've tried to tell him that I don't think we can be more than friends, but he won't listen.'

'You look like her, you know,' Elissa said suddenly.

'Like who?'

'Karen.'

Sara stared at her cousin in astonishment. 'You've met her?'

Elissa shook her head. 'Peter's shown me pictures of her. She's tall and slender and has blue eyes. There's a definite resemblance.'

Sara frowned and bit her lip. Wasn't it a bit odd that

Peter would be serious about a woman who looked like his first wife? Did it mean that he was trying to re-create his marriage in some bizarre way? 'I suppose it's not unusual,' she said hesitantly, 'for a man to be attracted to a certain type of woman. Physically, I mean, but I've often wondered . . .'

Just then the buzzer sounded, announcing that Lee had arrived and was waiting in the vestibule of the apartment building, and Sara picked up her coat and threw it over her arm.

'Now, don't do anything I wouldn't do,' Elissa warned.

Sara opened the door. 'How much leeway does that give me?'

'Just enough,' said Elissa with a grin, 'to get yourself into trouble!'

But there was nothing at all about the beginning of the evening that even hinted at trouble. Lee was a charming and considerate escort, handsome and elegant in a dark grey suit, his black hair brushed sleekly back. He complimented Sara on her dress, helped her with her coat and hailed a taxi with the expertise of a born and bred New Yorker. They went to a well-known restaurant where the atmosphere was subdued but luxurious and the lights dim enough so that Lee's presence didn't arouse too much attention and when he was recognised, the guests were far too sophisticated to act as if it mattered. Still, Sara was well aware that several of New York's most beautiful women had noticed their entrance into the restaurant and that admiring eyes were following Lee's wide shoulders as they made their way past discreetly placed ferns and tables covered with fine linen and cutlery.

Lee, she saw with a quick glance at his harsh profile, did not acknowledge either the admiration or the interest, but held one hand firmly under Sara's elbow as they followed the maître d'. She, however, couldn't forget the man she was with, and every curious glance from another woman reinforced her own sense of insecurity, giving her the feeling that, like the female bird of the species, she was the one whose plumage was dull and uninteresting.

They ordered dinner from large scroll-like menus with dishes written in flowing script, and their conversation throughout most of the evening was lighthearted and casual. They discussed the theatre over heart of palm salads, politics between bites of sole stuffed with crab, and the latest movies well into the dessert course of chocolate cheese cake, touching upon nothing controversial or disturbing until the after-dinner drinks were served.

'I think you're making a mistake,' Lee told her, lifting a glass of Grand Marnier to his lips.

'About what?'

'About not coming to rehearsals. We need you there.'

'I've said everything in the play,' Sara replied. 'It speaks for itself.'

Lee frowned, an expression that brought his dark eyebrows into a single harsh line over his deep-set eyes. 'There are many ambiguities in the play.'

She stirred some sugar into her coffee. 'Not in my mind.'

'It interests me that Maria is in every scene,' he said slowly. 'It means that you were writing only what you yourself heard.'

Sara kept on stirring, her eyes on the dark swirling liquid in her cup. 'I don't know what you're talking about.'

'All the dialogue in that play was things that were either said to you directly or that you overheard.'

She maintained an air of composure. 'Don't confuse fact with fiction. The play is not my life story.'

'No, but it's about you. About a girl of thirteen who stopped speaking because she thought that something she said had destroyed her parents' marriage.'

'And learned that it wasn't true,' Sara added sharply.

Lee twirled the small aperitif glass in his lean fingers. 'But en route to that knowledge, she was privy to several private conversations. Have you ever noticed how people react to those who are mute or inarticulate like little children? They act as if they aren't there.'

'If you're suggesting that my mother and my psychiatrist said things in front of me that were of a sexual nature,' said Sara, angry glints in her eyes, 'then you're on the wrong track.'

'Were you blind and deaf as well as dumb?' he murmured.

She was furious. '*Adjustments* is . . . is about nice people. It has a happy ending. Why are you trying so hard to twist it into some sort of dark drama?'

'Because that's what you've written,' Lee said curtly, putting his glass down on the table.

'Did you invite me to dinner to have this argument?' Sara said frigidly. 'If so, try my office next time. It's more conducive to that sort of thing.'

'I invited you to dinner,' he said in a voice that was only barely civil, 'because I'm curious about what makes you tick.'

Sara had the infuriating feeling that Lee considered her nothing more than a bug on a slide awaiting dissection. 'Then I'm afraid that you'll just have to keep guessing.' She picked up her evening bag. 'If you don't mind, I'd like to leave. It seems I've developed a headache.'

She knew that he did mind, but he was gentleman enough not to show it. The waiter arrived at the flick of his hand, and the bill was paid, although the maître d' kept insisting in a disgustingly servile manner that the restaurant was honoured, grateful and privileged to

have Mr Lee Cameron grace their establishment. By the
end of the exchange, the line of Lee's mouth was harder
than before and his anger was palpable in the air as
they came out of the restaurant's elegant wrought-iron
doors. Sara shivered a bit in the cold and buttoned her
coat higher around her neck, but there was nothing she
could do about the wind which tugged at her hair,
blowing copper strands across her mouth and cheeks.

'We'll catch a taxi,' muttered Lee as he noted her
shiver and stepped out into a crowd of people who had
just come out of a nearby movie theatre, pulling her
after him.

Neon lights flashed across the marquee of the theatre,
the wide windows of the stores on the street were
illuminated like daylight, and the oncoming traffic
threw its headlights into the crowd, making every face
visible and distinctive. Lee had just stepped forward off
the pavement to wave down a taxi when someone near
him exclaimed, 'Hey! Isn't that Lee Cameron!?'

There was a sudden shifting of the crowd as people
stopped walking and others turned towards the voice.

'It is Lee Cameron!' a female voice shrilled.

'You mean the guy in *Danger Zone*?'

Lee stepped back on to the pavement and grabbed
Sara, putting his arm around her and cursing under his
breath. Within seconds, they were surrounded by eager
faces, outstretched hands and bodies so close that
Sara's heart began to pound in her chest like that of a
wild animal surrounded by menacing hunters.

'The movie star . . .!'

'Can I have your autograph!?'

'Jeez, I can't believe . . .'

They were jostled and bumped, the centre of a crowd
that was growing in size, strength and determination.
Someone tried to catch hold of Sara's hand and pull her
away, but Lee turned her quickly in another direction.
The noise level grew so loud that she could barely make

out the words coming at her from the wide opened mouths.

'And who's she?'

'Gotta be someone important.'

'That red-haired actress on TV, that's who she is.'

A little old lady with no teeth and snake-like grey hair pushed her way to the front. 'I saw you, dearie, on *Love Boat*,' she cackled. 'I watch the show all the time.'

Sara huddled deeper into the curve of Lee's arm and felt the support of his strong body behind her. 'Hold steady,' he murmured into her ear. 'We're about to make a getaway!'

How could she hold steady when they were pushing at her, yelling at her and grabbing the cuff of her coat? Her teeth began to chatter and her knees felt so weak she thought she would fall if Lee let go of her. The worst came when she felt the fingers in her hair. She screamed when they snatched out her tortoiseshell combs and hairpins, causing her copper hair to tumble around her cheeks in wild disarray.

'Now!' ordered Lee.

He pulled her so hard that she would have completely lost her balance if he didn't have such a firm grip on her wrist. The crowd, surprised at Lee's sudden movement, parted before him. He ran with Sara behind him and they ducked into an alley and turned down another street and then another. The voices behind them became muted and then still as the crowd gave up the chase, and Lee finally stopped running and pulled her into the doorway of a closed store on a blessedly quiet and dark corner. They huddled together, breathing hard, the smoke of their breaths mingling in the air.

'My God,' Sara whispered, still shaking and terrified, her head against Lee's shoulder, her arms around his coated waist.

'Horrible, isn't it?' he said quietly, stroking her tangled hair.

'How can you live like this?' she exclaimed.

'With difficulty,' he said, and she could hear his teeth clenching.

Sara tried to stand on her own two feet, tottered in his embrace and then looked down. 'I've lost a shoe,' she said incredulously, staring at her left foot, bare except for the shreds that were left of her stocking.

'If it's any consolation,' said Lee with irony, 'they stole a glove and a button from my coat.'

'A button? Why would anyone want a button?'

They stared at one another, their faces white ovals in the dim illumination of a nearby street light, shadows formed by the planes and angles of nose, chin and eyes. Sara was the first to start laughing and then Lee joined in, his head thrown back, white teeth gleaming. They laughed helplessly, leaning against one another, gasping in the night air. It was either that or cry, Sara realised later, and they laughed instead; at their fears, at the trauma of it all, at how ludicrous it really was.

'A button,' Sara kept repeating. 'A Lee Cameron button!'

'They thought you were on television,' he said. 'On *Love Boat*, of all places!'

'They couldn't believe that you'd be going out with someone as ordinary and mundane as me.' And Sara started to laugh again.

Suddenly, his hand was cupping her cheek, his thumb forcing her chin up. 'You're not ordinary,' he said softly.

Sara blinked at the serious tone of his voice and stared into his shadowed face. He touched her eyebrow with one finger and then traced its arch to her temple. From there he caressed the length of her cheek, moving his hand down until he reached her mouth where he ran his fingertip over the width of her lower lip. Her lips trembled slightly and she sighed in gentle surrender to his change of mood, to the evocative sensation of that warm touch.

Lee bent his dark head as his hand slid to enclose her throat, keeping her face raised to his. Their lips met, moved on one another and then parted. Sara, lost in the sensations, moved blindly against him, reaching upwards with her arms to tangle her fingers in the thick strands of hair at his neck. Lee's mouth left hers and moved to her exposed throat where a pulse beat quickly in the rapid rhythm of a hummingbird's wings, and his lips moved against the tender silk of her skin.

'Not ordinary at all,' Sara heard him whispering, and her heart seemed to shift in its space, its already unsteady beat altering to something deeper and heavier. She didn't know what it was; only that it made her breath catch and her limbs feel weak. She was heedless of anything beyond the soft caress of his mouth and didn't recognise that irrevocable moment when her heart, previously empty and untouched, began that mysterious journey to love.

CHAPTER FOUR

THE roses began to arrive the following week. On Sunday, Sara received one rose, blood-red and fragrant, with an embossed card that simply read *Lee*. Monday brought two roses, white this time with delicate velvety leaves, their edges slightly curled. On Tuesday, the florist delivered three pale pink roses, on Wednesday four yellow ones. Thursday was five scarlet roses; on Friday when the doorbell rang, Sara and Elissa exchanged looks.

'You answer it,' said Sara. It was eight-thirty in the morning and they were both having breakfast. Sara was dressed already, but Elissa was still wearing her blue bathrobe and slippers. Her classes didn't begin until mid-morning.

She put down her piece of toast. 'Aren't you even curious? He must be running out of colours!'

Sara gave a helpless shrug. 'I'm sure he'll have thought of something.' She didn't quite know what to do about the avalanche of roses. The cool blue and white of her apartment had taken on a different air as the vases of flowers proliferated. Their fragrance gave the living room a heavy, musky scent; their vibrant colours added a disturbing and jarring note of intensity. For the life of her, Sara was unable to forget Lee's existence. Although he hadn't called her since their evening out, the roses were an insistent reminder of their embrace in the shadows, of his kiss and her own response.

It wasn't that she hadn't been kissed before, she thought as she poured herself another cup of coffee. She had been, many times, but never with quite the same sensual edge. She stirred some cream into the cup and added a teaspoon of sugar, her face pensive. She shouldn't have been surprised that Lee could evoke passion; he must be an expert in lovemaking. How old was he? Thirty-five and hardly celibate, a man who was accustomed to being with women who might even think it a deprivation to sleep alone. It made Sara feel slightly sick inside when she contemplated the way she had kissed him back, proving that she was certainly no different from his other women and possibly even more eager. No wonder she was getting bombarded with roses! She had set Lee on a course of seduction and he was strewing the path with flowers.

'Yellow and orange.'

'Hmm?' Sara looked up from her coffee.

Elissa had opened the long white box and was pulling the roses out from their bed of green paper and ferns as she walked into the kitchen. 'These are really beautiful. I didn't know that roses came in colours like this.'

They were magnificent; seven full blossoms whose petals were a deep yellow shaded with coppery salmon. Sara eyed them with irritation. 'We don't have another vase.'

Elissa buried her short nose into the flowers and took an appreciative sniff. 'I'll combine Tuesday's flowers with Wednesday's. Monday's rose has had it.'

'When will it stop?' Sara said with a sigh.

Elissa gave her an incredulous look. 'You don't want the roses?'

'No.'

'You must be out of your mind! It's so romantic.'

'Lee Cameron is not after romance,' Sara said coldly.

Elissa gave her a reproving smile. 'Tut-tut, cousin! Take your mind out of the gutter.'

'Well?' Sara challenged her. 'What exactly do *you* think Lee Cameron wants?'

Elissa shrugged and then sniffed at the roses again. 'Does it matter? He's doing it with such style.'

Sara grimaced and took a sip of her coffee. 'Anyway, I don't know why he's chosen me. There must be a million women out there who'd like a moonlight and roses affair with him.'

'Maybe he's interested in your mind.'

'Ha!'

Elissa took one more sniff of the roses and then regretfully laid them back in their box before sitting down at the table again. 'Come on, Sara, admit that you like all the attention.'

'It would be far more flattering,' she said drily, 'if he didn't just think of me as another female conquest.'

Her cousin took a bite of her toast, her eyes dreamy. 'I'm dying to be a female conquest,' she said.

'Really, Elissa, this isn't funny. The living room looks like a hothouse.'

'Methinks the lady doth protest too much.'

Sara leaned forward to add weight to her argument. 'I wouldn't get involved with Lee Cameron if he were the last man on earth.'

Elissa reflectively chewed on her toast. 'Famous last words.'

She sat back in surprise. 'You don't think I can hold him off?'

Elissa gave a noncommittal shrug.

'And besides, there's Peter.'

'You'd use him as a shield against Lee?' asked Elissa with a frown.

Sara spread her hands apart in a gesture of helpless entreaty. 'I didn't mean it that way. It's just that he's very much a part of my life.'

Elissa threw her a questioning glance. 'Is he?' she asked.

Sara blushed. 'Not in that way,' she said quickly, taking a sip of her coffee and reflecting that it wasn't for Peter's lack of trying. He was virile and masculine and he'd been urging her to go to bed with him for months. He pointed out, quite rightly, that they were both free, over twenty-one, and society no longer frowned at unmarried couples who engaged in sex. Sara had resisted, partially out of the sheer conservatism of her nature and partially out of a conviction that sex alone would be unsatisfying. She wasn't so old-fashioned that she thought that marriage had to come first, but she held a firm belief that love had to be present to make the experience successful.

Elissa buttered another piece of toast. 'He must be taking a lot of cold showers.' She gave Sara a grin. 'Saves on fuel costs.'

Sara ran distracted fingers through her hair, 'I wish I knew what to do about Peter.'

'I think we've had this conversation before.'

'Have we?' Sara gave her cousin a quick glance. 'I'm sorry, I don't mean to be so boring.'

'It's not boring. I'm getting a vicarious thrill out of your love life.'

'Omit the word *love*,' Sara said wryly, 'and you'll have it right.'

'Peter loves you.'

Sara's mouth turned down at the corners. 'I know, but I can't seem to love him back.'

'And Lee Cameron?' Elissa asked softly.

'Love doesn't even enter into the picture,' Sara retorted. 'He must be bored and looking for a bedmate.'

'You're pretty hard on him,' Elissa commented.

Sara's voice was sarcastic. 'His reputation proceeded him.'

'You must admit that he's classy though,' Elissa responded, then gave her a diabolical smile. 'He might come out of this smelling like a rose.'

Sara groaned. 'It's too early in the morning.'

'Sorry,' Elissa said, grinning, 'but I just couldn't resist it.'

Elissa might have classified Lee's gift of the roses as classy, but Sara considered it as a form of bribery, a belief strengthened when the long boxes of roses turned into tiny jeweller's ones, each bearing a small charm. She couldn't believe it when she opened the first with its small silver rose, but when the next one arrived, a tiny jade rose, and then the next, a gold one, she knew she couldn't bear it one minute longer. She angrily tucked the three charms into an envelope, stuffed them into her handbag and, during her lunch hour, went to the theatre. It didn't occur to her until she had paid the taxi driver and had stepped out on to the pavement that Lee had got her exactly where he wanted her.

She stood hesitantly outside the theatre door and contemplated, with growing dislike, Lee's manipulations. He had never phoned her after their evening; he'd just sent the roses and charms, daily and nagging reminders that he was a definite part of her life. Sara had grown frustrated because she couldn't figure out what he would do next and irritable because his motivations were so patently obvious. All along, she had been convinced that the gifts were his means of softening her up for a seduction. She'd been tempted several times during the past week to get his unlisted number in the office and give him a piece of her mind, but she had resisted every urge. Indifference seemed a more devastating tactic than any response could be. But when the gifts had gone up in value, Sara had been sure that Lee was merely escalating his attack, and her irritation had developed into a full-scale annoyance. He was going to learn, she had decided with determination, that she wasn't the kind of woman whose head was turned by expensive offerings.

But now it suddenly struck her that Lee had never intended a seduction at all and that the daily bombardment of gifts and her silent telephone had been part of a totally different kind of strategy. He had

invited her several times to watch a rehearsal, but Sara
believed that his so-called desire for her opinion merely
masked his real interest: Lee wanted her to see the play
in progress in the hopes that it would shock her into
talking about the past. She had, of course, refused to
come near the theatre, admitting only to herself that she
was terrified of her private demons being aroused at
seeing her own life portrayed by others. Yet here she
was, staring up at the empty marquee from under her
umbrella, ready to march beyond those heavy wooden
doors to do battle. With almost no effort whatsoever
and an amount of money that Sara knew was negligible
to a man of Lee's wealth, he had manoeuvred her right
into the lion's den.

Sara sighed, thought about retreating and then
shrugged her shoulders in defeat at the idea of finding
another taxi and returning to the office. Sleet beat
against her umbrella and rain dripped from the edge of
her umbrella down the back of her fawn raincoat.
February had ended on a dismal climatic note with
every day bringing some form of unpleasant precipita-
tion, and March didn't look any more promising. The
passing traffic sprayed slush up on to the sidewalks and
the buildings looked grey and grimy. The wind, cold
and damp, blew the strands of her hair against her face,
and she shivered, wishing that she'd worn a sweater as
well as a coat. Her fine wool dress, soft, blue and
clinging, was no barrier against the cold.

She walked around to the side door of the theatre,
presented her pass to the guard and tip-toed up a flight
of stairs and down a narrow corridor whose door came
out to the lobby of the mezzanine. Working for B.J.
gave Sara an advantage over other theatregoers. Not
only did she get free tickets to many Broadway shows,
she was also allowed access to backstage areas and
dressing rooms. She knew the layout of most of the
New York theatres like the back of her hand. She

walked down the darkened aisle to the front row of
seats in the mezzanine and sat down, leaning forward so
that she could see what was happening on the lighted
stage.

It was, she saw immediately, the opening scene of the
first act. Constance, with obvious nervous anticipation,
was arranging and rearranging a picture that hung over
a sofa. The set was designed to be a suburban living
room, typical and middle-class. There was a fireplace in
one corner, a bookshelf, knick-knacks, a carpet, a
couch and two flanking wing chairs. Constance dallied
with the picture, flicked non-existent dust off the sofa
arm, moved one of the wing chairs to a slightly different
angle and looked at her watch, not once but at least
half a dozen times. When a door slammed, off-stage,
her shock was obvious, the fear in the large, dark eyes
evident even to Sara, one balcony up.

'Maria, is that you?' she called out, her voice echoing
into the wide expanse of empty orchestra. The theatre
was absolutely silent and dark except for the stage. Sara
missed the rustle of an audience; the coughs, shuffling
and whispers. She was alone in the mezzanine, and on
each side of her the folded velvet chairs stretched in
long curving rows like a mute chorus.

She watched as Felicia entered, unaware of the small
tremor that ran through her at the actress's appearance.
Felicia had a slouch to her shoulders and a sullen look
on her face. She wore a pair of jeans and a dirty T-shirt;
her fair hair looked tousled and unkempt. If Sara
hadn't known better, she would never have guessed that
Felicia was any older than thirteen.

'How did it go, darling? Did you like Dr Holme?'
There was almost an hysterical edge to Constance's
voice, and Sara looked at her with appreciation. The
actress fitted the role of the suburban housewife
perfectly. She wasn't glamorous, but neither was she
unattractive. There was something about the way she

stood and moved her hands that suggested the desparation of a mother who had a rebellious teenage daughter.

Felicia ignored her and sat down on the couch, stretching her legs before her and staring at her sneakers.

John's voice came from the orchestra. 'Too mild, Felicia—much too mild. You've just been through your first session with Dr Holme. You didn't want to see him and you don't like what he said. You're about to take all your anger out on your mother.'

Felicia stood up. 'You want me to give the sofa a work-out?'

'Let the springs have it.'

'Okay,' she grinned.

The scene repeated itself with the same frightening tenacity of a nightmare. Sara leaned forward, her hands clutched together, her pulse pounding heavily in her throat. She watched Constance fiddle nervously with the knick-knacks and recognised her own mother in that tense figure. Felicia entered, flopped heavily down on the sofa, kicked the arm with one foot and then stared at her fingernails.

'Did you talk to him, dear? That's what I sent you for. To give you a chance to talk a bit and get some of your problems out.' Constance sat down in one of the chairs and then sprang up again to straighten a curtain. 'It helps to talk. It really does.' She looked around. 'Maria? Are you listening to me? Darling, please, I can't bear this silence.' Her hands reached out in a pleading gesture. 'Didn't Dr Holme tell you that it isn't good to keep everything inside? You'll . . .'

Sara was glued to her seat, rigid with tension. She had known that it would be bad, that seeing her words brought to life would bring back the old anguish, the anger and unhappiness. She remembered her first visit to the psychiatrist. She hadn't wanted to go and refused to until her Aunt Betty had intervened and begged her to try. And the first session had been horrible. The psychiatrist, the real Dr Holme, had said he was there to listen, and listen he had – to fifty minutes of unbearable silence. She had sat there sullenly, hating him and hating her mother. But he had seemed unconcerned, not caring how she wanted to spend the next hour. He smoked a pipe and contemplated the ceiling as if he had all the time in the world. When she had finally got home, her sullen silence had driven her mother's initial nervous concern into a screaming fit of fury and frustration.

Felicia had it down pat. Sara could remember the way she had slouched on the couch, staring at her hands and out the window, anywhere except at her mother, who was trying desperately to make some sort of contact. She could recall quite vividly how her muscles had strained to hold that seemingly careless pose and the effort it had taken to act as if she were not only dumb but deaf. Her mother's voice had ricocheted off the walls at her, beat against her eardrums with the forces of harsh, brutal waves. Sara was catapulted back into the past as Constance's voice rose in the empty theatre. Why didn't she understand that Sara couldn't talk? Why didn't they all leave her alone? Sara swallowed convulsively and a cold sweat broke out on her brow. What was wrong with silence? she wanted to scream back. Didn't her mother know that words were dangerous and could destroy people?

'So you've finally come.'

Sara was wrenched forcibly out of her agonizing memories to find Lee sitting beside her, his face a white oval in the gloom, his hair and eyes midnight black.

'Do you like it?' he continued.

Sara gave a shudder which she hastily concealed by fiddling with her handbag. 'They're very good.'

'Yes.' Lee turned his face towards the stage and for a

few seconds they watched Constance and Felicia play
out the scene. Constance was now pacing the stage,
vitriolic words pouring out of her, while Felicia with
marvellous command of body language responded in
attitudes that managed quite successfully to express
hostility, anger, confusion and unhappiness.

Unable to withstand the emotions that poured from
the stage, Sara stood up and pulled her coat around
her. She had completely forgotten what had brought
her to the theatre in the first place, and she only knew
that she had to get out quickly before she broke down.

Lee seemed to recognise her sudden urgency and he
stood up beside her. 'Come, we'll go for coffee,' he said,
placing his hand under her elbow. 'There's a little place
around the corner that's reasonable. They know me
there, so I don't get the big celebrity act.'

Sara blindly followed his lead out of the theatre and
into the coffee shop. She was dazed by their emergence
out into the grey, cold rain and then into the bright
lights of the restaurant. She barely noticed the booth as
they sat down and, when the waitress asked for her
order, she merely blinked in surprise.

'The lady will have a roast beef sandwich,' said Lee,
'and I'll have a cup of coffee and a Danish.'

Sara started to come alive. 'I'm not hungry,' she
protested.

'Nibble at it,' he ordered. 'It'll put the colour back
into your cheeks.'

Sara involuntarily raised her hand to her face as if
she could feel her pallor with her fingertips. 'I'm all
right,' she said.

Lee arched one dark eyebrow. 'I've seen you looking
healthier.'

'It . . . it was a shock,' she confessed.

Lee knew exactly what she was talking about. 'I
wondered if it would be,' he said, leaning back against
the cushion of the bench and watching her. He was

dressed in jeans and a dark blue cable-knit sweater with sleeves rolled up to reveal muscular forearms with a coating of dark hair. His dark hair was damp from the rain, its ends curling against his forehead. It gave him a boyish look that made Sara feel more comfortable. He didn't seem like the Lee Cameron who played the predatory hunter in *Danger Zone*.

'I don't think I'll go to any more rehearsals,' she said.

'Too painful?'

She nodded. 'I thought writing the play was cathartic, but I see there's one more step to go.'

Lee reached forward and took Sara's hand between his. 'Perhaps it's necessary,' he said gently.

His fingers caressed the sensitive chord at her wrist and his palms warmed her cold hand. The stroking seemed to reach within her and ease the troubled state of her heart. She yielded to it, her head bent so that the thick strands of her coppery hair hid her expression from Lee's watchful gaze. She had not realised how strong his impact on her could be. Tense as she had been in the theatre, she had trembled at the sound of his voice, its husky timbre cutting through the anger and despair she had felt as she listened to Constance. No man had ever affected her that way, and Sara was at a loss to understand her vulnerability in Lee's presence. She didn't like the way the touch of his fingers could make her feel so weak and languid.

The return of the waitress with their order caused Lee to let go of her hand, and she sighed with relief, sitting back and tucking her hair behind her ears. She picked up her sandwich and took a bite, suddenly realising that she was ravenous.

Lee talked for a while about the theatre, the weather and the life and habits of New Yorkers, inconsequential topics that were neither threatening nor upsetting. He talked until Sara was relaxed, the colour back in her cheeks, her blue eyes no longer frightened. When she had finished eating and the waitress had cleared the table, he gave her a smile. 'You've come to return the charms.'

Sara looked at him in surprise. About halfway through her sandwich she had remembered her reason for going to the theatre in the first place, but she no longer had a feeling of righteous anger. She'd been through too much emotion in the past hour to care any longer. Still, she hadn't expected Lee to bring the subject up. 'Yes,' she replied cautiously, 'I did.'

'You don't think they're suitable?'

'I don't usually accept gifts from strangers.'

Lee gave her a smile. 'Are we strangers?'

Sara sought for the right word. 'We're acquaintances,' she said at last. 'Business associates.'

'That has a cold ring,' he said wryly.

She opened her handbag and brought out the envelope. 'Here,' she said.

Lee took the envelope and spilled the charms on to the white formica table where the tiny blossoms glinted silver and gold, the jade rose's polished surface gleaming a dark green. 'I don't know many women who would have turned these down,' he said.

'I guess I'm different,' Sara said.

He eyed her shrewdly. 'Because of your past?'

She suddenly came to life. 'No,' she snapped. 'My past has nothing to do with the person I am today.'

Lee picked up the gold rose and held it in his dark, lean fingers, his thumb caressing its hard petals the way it had touched the soft inner skin of her wrist. 'Aren't we all the products of our past?' he asked softly.

Sara's mouth had gone dry as she watched his fingers and for a second she didn't realise that he was waiting for an answer. 'No ... yes,' she shook her head in confusion. 'I don't know.'

'I'm certainly one.'

She had read his publicity sheets. 'Small-town boy

makes good?' she asked incredulously. Lee's sophistication suggested that he had thrown off the influence of his boyhood and the years he had spent in a tiny midwest town of farmers and yokels.

His mouth turned into a bitter slant. 'A small town can be worse than an urban jungle,' he said.

Sara glanced at him in surprise. His publicity sheet had mentioned the small local school, sandlot baseball games, hayrides and high school football, and she had thought that Lee's childhood sounded idyllic, a version of the American dream. She had imagined a white-spired church, apple pies cooling on the sill and a neighbourly intimacy.

Lee caught her astonishment. 'Don't believe everything you read,' he said. 'My publicist has a way with words.'

'But your childhood sounded quite happy,' she protested.

'My parents fought for years until my father skipped town,' he said grimly.

'Skipped town? I thought . . .'

'That he was dead? As I said, my publicist has a way of twisting the truth for public consumption. He abandoned us, leaving us to live on the charity of neighbours and the town's benevolence. From the time I was ten, I was referred to as the Cameron boy—you know, the one without a father.' A small muscle moved in Lee's jaw. 'My mother couldn't hold her head up in public, and I vowed that I'd make enough money to get the both of us out of that lousy town if it killed me. I left home at eighteen for Hollywood and didn't go back until I could do it in style. The hypocrites couldn't wait to roll out the red carpet for me then.'

Sara now understood why Lee's movie roles had been so successful. The hard, ruthless streak in his character, developed through years of unhappiness, had combined with his dark good looks to give his screen personality an overwhelming masculine charisma. Sara had not been partial to thrillers, but even she had been able to recognise Lee's sensual magnetism. And it was all that much more appealing when she could envisage the small, hurt boy whose pride had forced him to assume a façade of swagger and toughness. She had an instinctual urge to caress the harsh line that ran from his nose to the bitter curl of his mouth as if she could soothe away the pain of his memories.

'Does your mother still live there?' she asked softly.

'God, no! I got her out as soon as I could afford it. She lives in Florida now and has remarried. He's a gentle man who treats her very well.'

'She must be very proud of you.'

Lee gave an unexpected grin and the tension lightened. 'My best fan,' he confessed. 'She has one room devoted to Lee Cameron memorabilia. The only thing she holds against me is that I haven't given her any grandchildren.'

Sara looked down. She didn't want to be reminded that Lee had had numerous women and no intention of settling down. She couldn't deny her attraction to him, and she knew it was fatal to get involved with a man whose amorous exploits filled the gossip columns. She wasn't in Lee's class at all; she was too vulnerable, too easily hurt.

'. . . perhaps that's why I wanted the role of Dr Holme,' Lee was saying, his voice reflective. 'I understand Maria; I've got first-hand experience in being abandoned by a father.'

Sara was stung. 'He didn't just walk out!'

Lee gave her a shrewd glance. 'What do you call it?'

'He had to leave. My mother wanted him to go.'

'He was innocent?'

'Of course he wasn't innocent,' Sara said angrily. 'No one was innocent.'

'That's what the psychiatrist proved to you?'

'I learned,' she said slowly, 'that there are two sides to every story.'

'But you still don't believe it, do you?'

She glared at him, angry that he was trying to provoke her and furious at herself for being manoeuvred into a position where he could pry into old but still painful wounds. 'I told you, I don't want to talk about my past,' she said coldly.

Lee leaned forward intently. 'I find the end of the play ambiguous.'

'Why? Maria talks again.'

'But I still get the feeling that she's antagonistic to the mother.'

'You have,' she said furiously, 'a bad habit of reading more into the play than I put there.'

'Still on the defensive?'

She glared at him. 'Only because you put me there.'

Lee shook his head as if he admired her tenacity of spirit. 'Why is it so important for you to separate the play from your own life? We both know it's about you.'

He was still holding the gold rose in his fingers, and now he put it back down on the table, its reflection catching Sara's eye. 'This was the reason behind the roses, wasn't it?' she said in a glacial tone.

He threw her a questioning glance. 'What?' he asked.

'You wanted to get me to the theatre, didn't you?' she challenged him. 'You hoped that seeing the play would cause me to talk about it.'

Lee deftly turned aside her attack. 'I think a beautiful woman deserves roses.'

'You must think I'm very naïve to believe a line like that,' Sara snapped.

Instead of being angry, Lee appeared amused. 'You don't think you're beautiful?' he asked.

Sara flushed. 'I'm not beautiful at all, and those roses were merely your way of trying to get some information.'

Lee took some time to study Sara's angry face. His dark eyes took in the thick waves of copper hair that framed wide blue eyes, a slender nose and a mouth with a full and sensuous lower lip. 'Perhaps,' he conceded musingly, 'not beautiful exactly, but intriguing.'

Sara's flush deepened from pink to scarlet. 'If you intend to insult me . . .' she began, beginning to slide out of the booth.

Lee leaned forward and easily pinioned her wrist so that she couldn't move. 'If you can't take gifts, compliments or insults then just how do I go about showing you that I'm interested, Miss Morrison?'

Sara sat perfectly still. 'Interested?'

He shook his head in disbelief. 'Subtlety doesn't work with you, does it?'

'If you're talking about an affair while you're here in New York, then you can forget it!' she snapped in a hot rush of words. 'I don't have any intention of . . .'

To her consternation, Lee began to laugh. 'I shouldn't have sent you roses,' he said. 'Thorns would have been more suitable.'

'You can't seduce me with gifts,' she said vehemently.

'I shouldn't have to *seduce* you,' he said. 'I was thinking along the lines of getting to know one another.'

He made her visions of licentious orgies seem ridiculous. 'Oh,' she said.

Lee raised an amused eyebrow as if he could read her thoughts. 'Did you think I wanted to take you immediately to bed?'

She couldn't help the expression that passed quickly across her face.

'It's not my usual practice,' he said drily.

'I thought . . . from the gossip columns . . .' Sara tried to stammer her way through a humiliating explanation.

'I told you, don't believe everything you read. The

press makes up liaisons that don't exist and can blow a casual date into a grand passion in five minutes flat.'

'What about Regina Delahunt?' Sara blurted out.

Lee's dark eyebrows met in a frown. 'Regina? What about her?'

'I saw her coming out of your room at the Hotel Moravia.'

He looked bored. 'Regina suffers from an intolerable case of celebrity-worship.'

'But you can't deny that there have been women . . .' Sara sought for the right words, 'in your life.'

Lee gave her a mocking smile. 'I'm not a monk,' he said, 'and the temptations have been many.'

Sara swallowed and looked down at the three miniature roses. 'I really don't want the charms,' she said.

He swept them nonchalantly off the table and put them in the pocket of his jeans. 'Why don't we start with dinner, then?'

'Dinner?'

'Your place or mine. I don't want a repeat performance of last time.'

'But I don't . . .'

Lee leaned forward and took the hands she was wringing together between his. 'There's something between us,' he said, his voice serious with no sign of its earlier derision. 'A spark, an attraction, call it what you want. I'd like to explore it, Sara, and find out exactly what it means. I can have a female in my bed by snapping my fingers, but you're not that kind of a woman. Let's go slowly and get to know one another.'

Lee would never know just how seductive his words were. Sara wasn't the kind of woman who could be swept off her feet and she was never reckless; it wasn't in her nature. Lee's suggestion of moderation appealed to her sense of restraint, and his arguments were so reasonable that she couldn't think of one opposing line of logic. She couldn't deny the spark of sensuality that flared between them; it made her pulse race when he was nearby and her bones felt as if they were made of water, but she never would have succumbed to Lee if he had tried to overwhelm her by lovemaking. She had carefully erected defences against casual or capricious sex, and he had obviously sensed it.

The slow approach with its built-in opportunities for calling a halt when things got rough or too fast appealed to her. She wouldn't have credited a man like Lee with that sort of sensitivity, but then he had surprised her in the past with his intelligence and perception, and she knew how prejudiced she had been against him. She still suspected that their opinions on *Adjustments* were as opposite as the poles, but she pushed away any suspicion that this approach was a new ploy to gain information about the play. She was tired of being distrustful and hostile; she wanted very much to be like Lee, and she wasn't unaware of the enviability of her position. Sara wondered how many women would give their right arms to be in her place, sitting opposite Lee Cameron in a utilitarian coffee shop and being offered the pleasure of his company, no strings attached.

If there was the faint ringing of cautionary bells in her mind, Sara ignored them and yielded to the sensation of Lee's hand on hers. He was holding her fingers, and she could feel the strength of his grasp. He had lean, masculine hands with a shading of dark hair on the back and muscular wrists, one of which was adorned with a gold-banded digital watch. As she gazed down at their entwined hands, Sara lost the thread of her thoughts, their essence drifting away like wisps of smoke from a dying fire. She only knew that she wanted to see Lee again in some place more private and intimate and that something new was stirring within her; a pleasurable warmth, a curl of desire, sensations that she had never felt before.

She shifted restlessly. 'My place,' she said.

Lee's dark eyes were on her lips. 'When?' he asked huskily.

'Friday?'

'I'll be there.'

CHAPTER FIVE

SARA stopped at D'Agostino's after work on Friday and shopped for dinner, feeling incongruously happy as she meandered down the aisles choosing such luxuries as artichoke hearts, filet mignon and a small box of strawberries, out of season and outrageously expensive. Cooking for Lee was going to be a different experience from cooking for Peter, who ate anything she put before him with stolid appreciation. The last meal she had given Peter was a hastily thrown together meat loaf and mashed potatoes with frozen peas. It wasn't his fault, she reflected as she wheeled her cart to the check-out, that Peter didn't bring out the best in her. It was just a symptom of the general malaise in the relationship. He was so complaisant that she often treated him with indifference, feeling terrible afterwards and chiding herself for not being more thoughtful to a man who supposedly adored her.

Sometimes she wondered if Peter hadn't merely got into the habit of loving her. He wasn't the type of man who would go out of his way to find a new date. He wasn't a partygoer or a man who thrived in a crowd. He preferred their quiet evenings together, believing that their serenity was a sign of compatibility rather than an indication that something was missing between them. Elissa's statement that Sara resembled his ex-wife, Karen, had piqued her imagination for a while, but nothing had come of it. Peter still remained Peter, sincere, kind, warm, generous and dull.

As she picked up her bag of groceries, Sara tried to decide what woman would be right for Peter. He needed someone who was lively and vibrant, and she acknowledged to herself that she was neither. She was quiet and contemplative, preferring to show the world a placid and imperturbable façade. She might know that still waters ran deep, and that strong and turbulent emotions buffeted her from time to time, but it was a knowledge she kept to herself. Only Lee Cameron had got a glimpse of the Sara that existed below the surface.

Lee . . . The thought of him stirred her as she picked her way through the crowded blocks on the way to her apartment, her handbag over one shoulder, the grocery bag on one arm. She'd found herself day-dreaming about him at work to the point that B.J. had wanted to know if she were ill, and when she said that she wasn't, he had shrewdly asked if Lee Cameron had anything to do with the breakdown of her efficiency. Someone at the theatre, it seemed, had noticed them leaving together and the news had travelled with a speed typical of gossip in acting circles.

Of course, she had had second thoughts since inviting Lee to dinner, and they had ranged from mere suspicions of his motivations to the heartfelt conviction that she, Sara Morrison, was an idiotic fool to believe that she could hold the interest of a man like Lee Cameron for more than five minutes; all of which led to the unhappy conclusion that she was being used in one form or another. Yet the idea of having Lee in her apartment gave her an undeniable shiver of anticipation which she recognised as a symptom of overwhelming physical attraction, and she had ruefully decided that Lee fell into that category of forbidden pleasures, heady but ultimately not good for your health. The fact that Peter, solid and reliable, didn't attract her while Lee, fickle and elusive, did merely pointed to a perversity that she supposed was typical of women. She had plenty of friends who had bypassed perfectly nice men for charming cads.

Sara reached her building, took the elevator up to her

apartment and began absentmindedly searching for the key in her bag as she walked down the corridor to her front door. Her thoughts were on the evening to come. She had to shower, change, fix the salad, and make sure there was tonic water for the drinks. 'Damn,' she muttered, pulling her bag closer to her and settling the groceries precariously between the wall and her leg. 'Where's that key?' She had to wash her hair, straighten the apartment and dig out her linen napkins . . .

The apartment door swung open. 'Thank heavens you're home,' she began, looking up in relief. 'I couldn't find my . . . Peter! What are you doing here?'

He didn't smile. 'Taking Elissa to a recital,' he said.

'Oh.' Sara hid her bemusement by picking up the groceries and walking past him into the apartment, noticing as she did that Peter was dressed in a dark grey suit and silvery blue tie and that his shaggy brown hair had been slicked down so that he looked almost handsome.

He followed her into the kitchen. 'I didn't know,' he said slowly, leaning against the doorjamb, 'that you liked to hobnob with celebrities.'

Sara shrugged off her coat, threw it over a chair and began to unpack the groceries. She had hoped in a half-hearted way that Peter could be left in the dark about her evening with Lee, but she had known that he would find out sooner or later. He had asked her to a movie tonight, but she had turned him down, saying that she was busy. Elissa, it seemed, had filled in the blanks.

'It's . . . business,' she replied lamely. 'We have to talk about the play.'

'I see.'

'Lee and I . . . we have differing views on Dr Holme's role. I thought it would be a . . . a good idea if we hassled them out during dinner.'

Peter didn't look convinced. 'He wants to come here?' he asked with a touch of sarcasm.

Sara deliberately avoided returning his gaze and placed the strawberries in the sink. She knew he was jealous, and she had the guilty feeling of being in the wrong although she had never actually committed herself to Peter or promised him anything beyond dates and home-made dinners. 'I invited him,' she said. 'He didn't seem to mind.'

Peter took a step forward, a scowl on his face. 'Sara, I hope you aren't crazy enough to think that a man like Lee Cameron would have the slightest . . .'

'Strawberries! What an extravagance!' Elissa sauntered into the kitchen and peered into the sink. 'Did you rob a bank? Or take out a mortgage?' She glanced at Sara's averted face and then noticed Peter's sullen look. 'Oops,' she said. 'Did I interrupt something?'

Sara gave her a strained smile. 'Not really. Peter was just wondering why I invited Lee to dinner.'

'Business,' Elissa said quickly. 'One of those casual business dinners with strawberries and . . . holy cow, filet mignon! Honestly, Sara, do I have to star in a movie? You've been keeping me on bread and water and spaghetti.'

'Lee Cameron,' Peter began, his mouth in a hard line, 'has a reputation with . . .'

Elissa, moving quickly to lessen the tension, took his arm and batted her eyelashes at him. 'Don't be jealous, darling,' she said in a seductive tone. 'You have me!'

He looked down at her and gave her an unwilling grin. '*You* could use a spanking.'

'Mmm, kinky,' she said, giving him a come-hither look that sat incongruously on her freckled, snub-nosed face.

Peter reached out and ruffled her fiery red curls. 'Come on, Elissa,' he said teasingly. 'You'd think a Sunday drive was kinky!'

'Hah! I'm beyond the age of consent, you know.'

'Consent to what?'

'I plead the Fifth,' Elissa protested. 'I don't want to incriminate myself.'

'You mean,' he asked in mock-disbelief, 'that you've graduated beyond the birds and bees?'

'Are you suggesting that I'm a woman without experience?'

Peter grinned. 'Sweet twenty and never been kissed.'

'For your information, I've been kissed thoroughly and on several occasions.'

'Uncles, brothers and cousins.'

'He's a nasty, isn't he, Sara?' Elissa said in reproach. 'Very nasty.'

Sara turned to find Peter giving her cousin an affectionate look, and she smiled at them both, thankful for Elissa's intervention and the way she had of lightening Peter's moods. She had never seen Peter get angry before and she didn't know the potential force of his fury. It struck her that he was the kind of man who had a slow-burning fuse with the capability of really blowing up if he were pushed too far. She shivered a bit and then shrugged the thought away. One dinner with Lee Cameron couldn't possibly qualify as a detonator for Peter's temper.

They left after that, and Sara saw them off at the door, thinking how charming Elissa looked in a silky dress that was the colour of mulberries and cut so simply that it made her rounded figure look almost slender. As she threw the bolt behind them, she wondered why Elissa didn't date more. Her cousin was cute and vivacious with a bubbly personality and an ability to flirt that Sara found enviable. She approached life with a devil-may-care attitude, only turning serious when it came to her music. In that sphere, she was ambitious and dedicated.

Sara frowned and decided that Elissa's problem lay in her attitude towards school and her music. She was far too serious and possibly so competitive that she didn't attract men in her own field, the ones that she met on a daily basis. What Elissa needed was exposure outside of school, and as Sara walked towards her bedroom, she promised herself that she would make an effort to include her cousin in her social life and introduce her to some new people. She knew that Elissa would resist; she fought anything that took her away from the long hours of cello practice that she claimed were necessary if she were ever to be a success. Sara sighed as she threw open her closet doors. It had always seemed strange to her that Elissa, former tomboy and prankster, had developed such a streak of devotion and ambition to music. She didn't understand it, but she also couldn't help admiring her cousin's discipline and the way she had channelled all that energy into the cello. What Elissa needed, she finally decided, was a steady man rather than a riotous social life; someone who could balance her fervour with calm affection and support.

An hour later, the filet mignon was ready for cooking, the shortcake had been made and the table in the living room alcove was set with fine white linen, gold-rimmed bone china, pale blue napkins and candles set in delicate brass holders. Sara made an adjustment in the placement of a tulip-shaped wine goblet and tilted her head to one side as she surveyed the table. She was wearing a smoky grey cashmere sweater with a turtleneck collar and a slender-fitting pair of black wool slacks. Her hair had been washed and brushed until it gleamed as red-gold as the flames that flickered in the candles.

When the buzzer rang, announcing that Lee was in the foyer and about to come up, Sara quickly straightened and nervously wiped her hands on her apron before taking it off and hanging it on a kitchen hook. She ran a comb quickly through her hair and checked her face in the mirror to make sure that her make-up, a bit of eyeshadow and lipstick, had not smudged. She grimaced at her own image, annoyed at the way her pulse was racing and her hands were trembling. She absolutely hated getting into such a flap over a man; it wasn't like her, and the feeling made her uncomfortable and irritable. By the time the doorbell rang, she was unconsciously scowling, the first thing Lee noticed when he walked in.

'Sweets for a sweeter expression?' he asked, one black eyebrow arched, as he handed her an elegant box of chocolates wrapped in silver paper. He was wearing grey slacks that emphasised the long length of his legs and the narrowness of his hips. A white shirt was unbuttoned to reveal the tanned column of his throat, and he had thrown a navy blue blazer over one broad shoulder.

Sara aimed for a pleasant smile, a small white lie and a remnant of her lost poise. 'Sorry, but I was afraid I'd burnt something,' she said, taking the chocolates and wishing that Lee wasn't quite so handsome, so tall and so overwhelmingly masculine. When she wasn't in his presence she could be objective about his motives, but when he was near her, she could no longer remember all the reasons why she should remain cautious, careful and clear-headed. The future no longer mattered when Lee stood by her, only the moment when, if she had so dared, she could reach out and touch his hand or the lean line of his jaw or his hair where it waved on his forehead.

He leaned forward and brushed her mouth with his. 'Smells good to me,' he said.

'I hope,' she said breathlessly, 'that you like strawberry shortcake.'

He gave her a long, lazy smile. 'My favourite,' he said softly.

They ate by candlelight, and Lee was appreciative and lighthearted. His high spirits were catching, and

Sara found herself laughing at his jokes about Hollywood and offering him ones about B.J. and the entertainment business. The candles flickered between them, casting a golden glow over the table, the flames reflected and glittering back at them in the crystal glasses and the burnished silver flatware. Music played softly from the stereo and the lights in the living room were dim. Sara had the lovely feeling that she and Lee were all alone on a ship, sailing nowhere in particular, an aimless and careless drifting in the sea of night where nothing mattered except his voice and smile and the look he gave her as if she was the only woman in the world.

After dinner, Lee wouldn't let her clean up the dishes, but led her to the couch where he pulled her down next to him, wrapped his arm around her waist and tucked her in close to his side. 'I don't like my women in the kitchen,' he said.

'Chauvinist,' said Sara, her eyes closing as she let her head rest against his shoulder, enjoying the scent of his masculine cologne.

Lee rested his chin on her head. 'It has nothing to do with chauvinism. I watched my mother cooking and cleaning in too many kitchens. That's how she supported us.'

His voice held a note of bitterness and Sara took his free hand and laced her fingers through his, hoping that he could feel her rush of sympathy. 'That must have been a hard way to live.'

He was silent and then he shifted slightly as if to shrug away the memories. 'Enough about me. Talk about Sara.'

She took a deep breath. 'I grew up in a small town on Long Island. My parents divorced when I was fourteen and when I finished high school, I got a job with B.J. I love working for him and I'm still there.'

Lee waited.

'Really,' she said, 'that's it.'

'Was your adolescence filled with a) trauma, b) embarrassment, c) acne, d) crushes, or e) none of the above?'

Sara laughed. 'None of the above.'

He pulled away from her a bit, unlaced his fingers from hers and tilted her head so he could look at her. 'Impossible,' he said. 'No adolescent survives unscathed. You're hiding something.'

She shook her head. 'Nothing. I was a very quiet teenager.' She didn't think it would be possible to convey her feelings during those years. The divorce and her response to it had separated her from her peers, and she had had few friends and no dates. When she looked back, she saw herself as insulated from those around her, wrapped in an emotional cotton wool, her routine carried out in a haze of isolation.

Lee looked into her eyes for a long minute and then glanced around the room at the muted blue furniture, the colour darker in the shaded lamplight, the plain white walls and the window covered only in white shades, its severity offset by a lush green fern whose branches almost reached to the floor. 'Your surroundings suit you,' he said musingly. 'Quiet, cool.'

'That's the way I am.'

'No love affairs? No heartbreaks?'

Sara shook her head.

'No boy-friends?'

'Of course I've had boy-friends,' she protested.

'Anyone in your life at the moment?' he asked casually.

'Nosy, aren't you?' she asked him, reaching up to tweak the appendage in question.

Lee grabbed her hand and brought it to his mouth. 'Well?' he asked, his lips on her wrist.

She shivered as his tongue touched her delicate skin. 'Well what?'

His voice was serious. 'Don't play with me, Sara. I want to know.'

She looked away from the dark intensity in his eyes. 'There is someone,' she admitted reluctantly.

'And . . .?'

'He's a banker. We've been dating for about six months.'

'You're lovers?'

'Lee!' Sara struggled to move out from the circle of his arm, but he wouldn't let her loose. 'You can't ask questions like that!'

'Why not?' he growled, pulling her closer to him until she put her hand to his chest in resistance.

'Because . . . it's none of your business!' Sara could feel the hardness of his muscles beneath her palm and the steady beat of his heart drumming against her fingertips.

His eyes narrowed, glinting between the black lashes. 'When I'm interested in a woman, everything about her is my business.'

'My relationship with Peter is private,' Sara insisted.

The steel grip of Lee's arm loosened so that she could sit back. 'You don't trust me, do you?'

'You're an attractive man,' she said slowly. 'You can have any woman you want. I . . . don't want to be another notch in your belt.'

'Sex doesn't have to be a one-way street,' he said softly. 'It can be a mutually pleasurable arrangement. Hasn't your Peter taught you that?'

Sara looked away from his keen glance, flushing at his assumption that she and Peter were lovers. She didn't want to discuss Peter with Lee, and she sought for another, seemingly less dangerous topic. 'How are rehearsals going?' she asked quickly.

Lee gave a mocking smile, an acknowledgment of her tactic. 'Great.'

'Have you . . . discussed your part with John?'

'John and I are in agreement about my interpretations,' he said smoothly.

She sat up in shock, pushing him away, her heart starting to knock erratically in her chest, her breath coming short. 'About everything!?'

He nodded. 'Yes.'

'Does he think that Dr Holme is ... having an affair with the mother?'

'He thinks it's obvious.' Lee saw the horror growing in her eyes. 'Sara ...' he began.

'And ... that there are ... sexual feelings between Maria and the psychiatrist?'

'Sara, it's as plain as the nose on ...'

'But I talked to him!' her voice rising in hysteria, tears springing into her eyes. 'I told him what happened. There was nothing like that. Nothing!'

'There must have been,' Lee said gently, 'but you've repressed it all.' He reached up to caress her cheek, but Sara roughly pushed his hand away.

'*You* talked John into it!' she hissed at him accusingly.

He shook his head. 'I'm sorry, Sara, but everyone can see it.'

'Even Constance and Felicia?' Her eyes were wide and entreating, begging him to say it wasn't true, their blue darker under the shimmer of unshed tears.

'I'm sorry,' he said softly.

'Oh God, I don't believe it,' she moaned, and buried her face in her hands, wondering in desperation why no one believed her, why they couldn't see the play for what it was—a story about a girl who needs to grow up and learn how the adult world works. Instead, they were twisting the story all around, weaving in undercurrents of sex that had never existed. The thought of thousands of people watching such a distorted version of her life was like a nightmare.

Lee forced her hands away from her face and lifted

her chin so she had to look at him, her eyelashes spiky and wet. 'Darling, this is crazy. You have to find out the truth or you'll be in agony. Why don't you talk to your mother and confront her with it?'

Sara sighed. 'It's not so easy. She doesn't live here. She's remarried and lives in Washington.'

'Your father?'

'He has another family, too. In California.'

'Do you keep in touch with either of them?'

'Rarely.' It was a short word and one that didn't begin to convey the bitterness that Sara felt towards both her parents.

'A relative, maybe. Someone who remembers what happened?'

She shrugged. 'Maybe it doesn't matter,' she said dully.

'Of course it matters,' he snapped. 'You can't spend the rest of your life walking around in an emotional vacuum because you can't face the past!'

Sara was stirred to anger. 'Who said I can't face the past?'

'I say it. Look at this room!' He waved his arm in an all-encompassing motion. 'Is this the room of a woman who can let her feelings go?'

A blinding fury shook her. 'That's what you've wanted all along, isn't it? A woman who will throw all her inhibitions to the wind and jump into bed with you?'

Lee's anger was no less volcanic for its coldness. 'At least it would prove that she has feelings,' he said icily.

'And I'm cold because I won't have sex with you at the drop of a hat!' Sara hissed.

'Have I asked you to sleep with me?' he grated.

'Isn't that what all the sweet talk was about? *Let's go slowly and get to know one another,*' she quoted back to him, her voice dripping with sarcasm. 'I'm not such a fool.'

His teeth clenched together. 'I dislike having my words twisted and distorted. That's not what I meant and you know it.'

'I know nothing more than that you came to New York to star in *my* play and ruin it!'

'Your interpretation of *your* play would ruin it,' he said coldly. 'It would be as meaningless as a lump of clay.'

'B.J. loved it,' she retorted.

Lee stood up angrily and glared down at her. 'For your information, B.J. introduced the play to me as, and I quote, *a story about repressed adolescent sexuality*, unquote.'

Sara felt as if she were strangling. 'He didn't,' she said slowly, rising to face him.

'Oh, yes, Sara, he most certainly did.'

They stared at one another for a long moment, his dark eyes angry, her wide blue ones disbelieving. Sara discovered that she was shaking and she had to clench her hands together to stop their trembling. 'You're lying,' she said.

'Wake up, Sara, before you drown in your own delusions.'

'The only delusion I ever had,' she said, her voice glacial, 'was that you and I could be friends.'

'No,' he said, his voice low. 'We could never be friends.'

Her chin lifted. 'So even you see it's impossible.'

His arm reached out and pulled her towards him even as she protested and tried to struggle away, her body rigid and unbending. 'Passionate lovers,' he murmured, 'or bitter enemies, but never anything so mundane as friends.'

'Let me go!'

His dark head bent over her and Sara shut her eyes to blot out the sight of his mouth coming closer, that mouth with its line of hard sensuality. A shiver began deep within her and her anger dissipated like fog under a hot sun. Without realising it, she arched towards him, bending back over the curve of his arm so that the points of her breasts touched his chest, the nipples swollen and taut against the light mesh of her bra. Pliable and yielding, her body sought union with his and when their hips met, thighs touching, Sara felt desire snake through her, an insidious and languorous weakness that arose from a pulsating ache in the very centre of her being.

'It's for you to decide.'

Her eyes snapped open to find Lee staring down at her, the glint of fire in his dark eyes belying his cool tone. She saw that he knew quite well what she had experienced in his arms, and she could feel his own arousal hard against her. Reluctantly she loosened her grip from his upper arms, the feel of his muscles imprinted on her fingers. 'Decide what?' she asked shakily.

'Lovers or enemies, Sara. I don't want anything in between.'

Sara didn't sleep for hours after Lee had gone, and she awoke the following morning with a pounding headache that put her back in bed for the afternoon. Their conversation ran through her mind like a broken record, repeating certain words and phrases over and over again —*You're lying. You have to find out the truth.—Lovers or enemies. You have to decide.* She couldn't think rationally; the pain in her head had a way of splintering her thoughts into incoherent pieces. The only thing that stood out, clear and whole against the confusion in her mind, was Lee himself. She couldn't forget his charm at dinner, the warmth she had felt in his arms, the anger he had inspired and then that devastating rush of desire that forced everything else out of its path like some inexorable force.

Sara cringed at the memory of the things she had said and the way she had acted. She had told Lee she didn't want to be another notch in his belt and then proven, beyond a doubt, that she would probably be his easiest conquest. What was it about Lee that caused her restraint to melt away like ice on a hot day? Why was she so susceptible to his particular brand of charm and masculinity? She had never gone for the type of man Lee personified; she didn't like men who were macho, tough and sexy. Or at least, she hadn't in the past.

Sara sat up, groaned at the stab of pain in her left temple, and dunked the cloth she had placed over her head into the small bowl of water that sat on her nighttable. She lay back, letting its cold dampness soothe her forehead, and thought about some of Lee's remarks. He had said that she didn't trust him, and Sara couldn't fault his perception, but how could she put her faith in a man who was known for his legion of lovers? She had gone through B.J.'s clippings on Lee and found that his tastes ran to long-legged blondes with high cheekbones and deep cleavages. Since Sara was not blessed with anything of these except for a pair of nice legs, she found it hard to believe that Lee saw anything desirable in her. Perhaps, she thought with a touch of irony, he really was more interested in her mind than in her body. She was an enigma to him, a woman who couldn't understand her own past.

She shifted restlessly in her bed as she thought about the play. She was no longer so sure of her own memories as she had led Lee to believe. The number of people who agreed with his interpretation of *Adjustments* had caused a small crack to appear in her confidence. Was she wrong about the past? Had she been blind to what had been going on around her? Sara tried to remember, shifting through memories and searching for hints that her mother had been having an affair with the psychiatrist, but the harder she tried, the more that time of her life seemed to be hidden from her. It was like walking through a thick grey fog and trying to discern the dark shapes at the edge of her vision.

How had she written the play in the first place? she wondered. If she couldn't recall anything now, where had the play come from? She had the suspicion that Lee would say that it had evolved from her unconscious, that those deeply buried memories had surfaced and driven her to write *Adjustments*. Most of it had been written in a white heat of intensity, and it now occurred to her that she hadn't really known what she was writing. It had poured out of her in a stream of remembered phrases and events. Perhaps her conscious mind had screened the memories and selected only the least suggestive for the play. Perhaps, despite her best efforts, reality had crept in.

Reality . . . the word caught in Sara's mind. For the first time, she thought seriously of finding out what had really happened. Perhaps her version was the real one; perhaps Lee's was. She would certainly never know if she buried her head in the sand like some long-necked ostrich. Did she have the nerve, she wondered, to search out the truth?

A door opened and a flood of light fell across the bed. Sara blinked and closed her eyes in pain. 'Elissa?' she asked.

'Sara! What's the matter?'

'A migraine.'

'You haven't had one of those in months.'

'Could you close the door, please.'

'Sure.' The door closed and Sara opened her eyes, thankful for the gloom. She saw Elissa sitting on the edge of the bed, her eyebrows in a worried knot. 'How long have you been this way?' her cousin asked.

'Since this morning.'

'I thought you were sleeping in and I had to go to school for an orchestra rehearsal.'

Sara propped another pillow under her head so that she wasn't flat on her back. 'Did Peter like the recital?'

Was it her imagination that Elissa didn't want to look at her? 'He might learn to like piano concertos some day,' she said lightly, then changed the subject. 'How did your dinner go?'

It was Sara's turn to look away. 'Fine.'

There was a short silence and then Elissa spoke. 'Can I get you anything? An aspirin? A glass of water?'

Sara shook her head, but only slightly. A movement any more forceful would make her brain feel as if heavy iron balls were rolling around inside, crashing against her skull. 'Elissa, do you remember anything about my parents' divorce?'

'Not much. I was only nine at the time.'

'I was just wondering if *Adjustments* was accurate. If it really happened the way I thought it did.'

Elissa gave her a knowing look. 'I take it that you and Lee are not in agreement about the play.'

It was hard to say, but Sara managed to get the words out. 'He thinks that my mother had an affair with the psychiatrist.'

'Aunt Marion?'

'It sounds ridiculous, doesn't it?' Sara gave a disparaging laugh.

Elissa shrugged. 'No crazier than your father sleeping with the librarian.'

Sara sat up, uncaring that pain rocked her head in waves. 'What are you talking about?'

It was Elissa's turn to look surprised. 'I thought you knew that.'

'Knew what?'

'That your father had been having an affair with Miss Dukes.'

'Before or after the divorce?' asked Sara, a sick feeling persisting in her stomach. She had loved her father with all the fervour that a little girl can bring to the only man in her life. She had been so hurt when he had left them; she had felt as if part of her had been cut away, and the pain and grief had been that much keener since she was convinced that it was her fault.

Elissa gave her a look of sympathy. 'Before, during and after.'

'How do you know?'

'My mother told me when I was old enough to be curious. Your parents hadn't got along for years—you know that.'

'I know, but I always thought ...' Sarah's voice trailed off. Her parents' fights had been loud and audible, part of the background noise of her childhood. She had been well aware that her father wasn't happy, but with the egocentric viewpoint of a child, she had never imagined that he had looked to another woman for comfort. It didn't hurt to think that he had been unfaithful to her mother, but it hurt like hell to think that he had been unfaithful to *her*, that he had given some of his love to someone else, even before he had left for California.

'Miss Dukes,' she murmured in disbelief.

'None other.'

'She always seemed so prim. Do you remember those glasses she wore?'

'I think she might have had a nice figure under those shapeless suits.'

Sara sighed at the image of her tall, handsome father and Miss Dukes. 'It's incredible.' Her world had shifted off its axis at Elissa's words and was now tilting at a crazy angle. If her father had been having an affair with Miss Dukes, then anything seemed possible. She wondered how he had managed to carry on the liaison without her mother knowing. Or had she known all along? She shook her head in confusion. Why had she been kept in the dark for so many years?

'Why don't you visit Mom?' Elissa suggested as she

noted Sara's expression. 'She'd be able to tell you what you want to know.'

'Would she tell me?'

'Why shouldn't she? It's a dead issue as far as anyone else is concerned.'

'I hate to bother her with . . .'

'Nonsense,' Elissa said heartily. 'You know my mother loves to see you and it's only a short train ride away. You could go tomorrow.'

'Will you come?'

Her cousin shook her head. 'Not me,' she said. 'I'll get questions about how I do my laundry and if I'm eating properly.'

Sara wavered, the pain in her head making her hesitant. 'Maybe . . .' she began, but Elissa cut her off.

'Go,' she said, and then in an odd echo of Lee's words, she added, 'You should find out the truth, Sara. You'll be unhappy if you don't.'

CHAPTER SIX

SARA'S widowed aunt, Betty Morrison, lived on the north shore of Long Island, about an hour away from Manhattan on the train. Her house was down a narrow, heavily treed lane that led to the Sound, and Sara had many memories of biking to her aunt's house in the heat of the summer and then walking five minutes further to reach the small, secluded beach that served the neighbourhood. The house was made of white shingle and had a wide veranda with an old wooden swing that had been the plaything of many Morrison children. It was a vintage house, well worn and lived in, with large rambling rooms and big, old-fashioned furniture more memorable for comfort than for style. Sara had always loved it and her aunt, who was slightly eccentric, colourfully opinionated and inclined to use less than savoury language. Whenever her parents had been fighting or carrying on a silent cold war, Sara had escaped to visit her aunt, who had muttered imprecations, enfolded her in a bear hug and fed her homemade chocolate chip cookies.

'It's about time you visited,' her aunt commented, opening the front door at Sara's knock. 'You haven't been around since the last time I killed the cat.'

Sara hugged her aunt's more than ample frame. 'Killed the cat?' she echoed.

'Metaphorically speaking,' said Betty. 'The damn thing thinks she owns the place. If she isn't sitting on my newspaper, she's sleeping on my pillow.'

'Which cat is this?' asked Sara, following her aunt into the living room where five cats of different colours snoozed in various locations, their bodies curled into tight, furry balls.

'Sheba, the Queen of,' Betty replied, picking up one black cat by the scruff of the neck and scowling into its sleepy face. 'Scat—and stay off my pillow!' She dropped the cat to the floor where it landed and lazily licked one paw. 'Scoot! Amscray! Hit the road!'

The cat waited while Betty sat down and then jumped up and settled in her lap. 'Damn thing,' she muttered, her hand idly stroking its curved back. 'Sit down, Sara. Don't stand on ceremony.'

Sara obediently sat at the end of the couch, the only place that wasn't occupied by books, magazines and felines. The living room held a dusty but pleasant disarray. It was dotted with knick-knacks, stacked with printed matter and the rug, its floral pattern almost completely worn away by age and cats' claws, sat slightly askew, its underpad sticking out in one corner. In front of her on the dented coffee table was a tray with mugs of steaming hot coffee and slices of fragrant banana bread. Her Aunt Betty wasn't much of a housekeeper, but she'd always been a fabulous cook.

'Now what brings you to this neck of the woods?' Her aunt sat back in her chair, crossed her arms over the prow of her breasts and gave Sara a severe look from her blue eyes. She was a big woman with curly greying hair, a round face underscored by a double chin, and a short nose that held up a pair of granny glasses. Elissa looked like a smaller version of her mother, but she had her father's colouring. Her father and Sara's were brothers.

Sara reached for a coffee. 'A Sunday visit.'

'Hah!'

'The pleasure of your company?' Sara ventured.

'I'm not senile yet,' Betty snorted.

Sara gave her a smile. 'Some banana bread and a bit of advice?'

'Now we're getting somewhere. It takes trouble to unglue you girls from Manhattan. So tell me what's going on. A man?'

Sara sipped her coffee. 'Not exactly.'

'Either a man is exactly or he's not. Pass me a piece of banana bread. I lost two pounds last week and I miss 'em.'

'I wrote a play about my parents' divorce.'

'First the man,' Betty insisted. 'Start at the beginning.'

'His name is Lee Cameron.'

'Lee Cameron ... Lee Cameron. It strikes a bell. Hold on a sec while I think. The movie star, that's it!'

'He's starring in a play that I wrote,' Sara explained.

'I thought you already had a beau. That Peter whatshisname.'

'Gray. You met him.'

'Not for you,' said Betty, shaking her head firmly. 'Not the right man at all. Nice, but he lacks pezzazz, and you could use a little of that.'

Sara had quite forgotten the circuitous route that a conversation with her aunt could take. The rules and regulations that accompanied normal adult discourse had to be thrown to the winds in Betty Morrison's presence. She followed a logic that was peculiarly her own and you had no choice but to go along for the ride.

'Anyway,' she began, 'Lee decided to take the role of the psychiatrist in the play . . .'

'A sexy man,' her aunt said. 'Very sexy. And lots of female friends, I gather.' She waved at a pile of newspapers under a side table, and Sara remembered that her aunt was a voracious reader and subscribed to dozens of magazines and periodicals, giving her a wide and eclectic knowledge of some highly improbable subjects.

Sara took a bite of banana bread and murmured appreciatively, 'This is delicious.'

Her aunt took an experimental bite. 'Not bad,' she said disparagingly. 'Trying to add you to his collection?'

Sara tried to ignore her. 'Lee and I don't quite agree about his interpretation . . .'

Betty tilted her head and gave her an appraising glance. 'I'd aim for a short, brief and intense love affair. I'm sure he's good in bed.'

'Aunt Betty!'

'Thought that would shock you,' her aunt said with satisfaction. 'I swear the young are more conservative than you'd think.' She took another bite and chewed ruminatively. 'Seriously, though, he could be a bit dangerous. On the other hand, you're not the type to get carried away. An interesting mixture, I'd say.'

Sara capitulated. 'I don't think I can afford to get involved with him.'

Her aunt gave her a knowing look. 'You could lose your heart? Or have you already?'

Sara kept the smile on her face. 'He's very attractive and very charming, but I'm still on the right side of sanity.'

'Hmmm. So he's taken the part of the psychiatrist and you think he's giving the play sexual overtones.'

Sara nodded and gave her aunt a smile of relief. She had also forgotten just how sharp Betty was. For all the twists and turns of the conversation, her aunt had not missed a clue, and she had made an intuitive leap to a conclusion that hit the nail on the head.

'And you don't much like it,' said Betty.

'Lee says that my mother was having an affair with the psychiatrist while I was in treatment.' Funny how the words came more easily the more she spoke them. It was almost as if she was getting used to the idea, reconciled to it.

Betty stuck out a pensive lower lip. 'Well, I don't know anything for definite. Marion and I were never great friends. You just might call it a suspicion.'

Sara let out the breath she was holding in. 'But you think it might have happened?'

'Does it shock you?'

'When he first suggested it, I thought he was crazy . . . I couldn't believe it.'

'But now you do?'

'Now, I think it might have been possible. Dad had left and she was all alone and not very happy.'

Betty leaned forward. 'Marion wasn't the type of woman to be without a man. You know that, don't you?'

Aghast, Sara stared at her aunt. 'Are you saying that there were other men . . . even before the psychiatrist?'

'Your parents' marriage was on the rocks the day after the wedding. I'm surprised it lasted as long as it did.'

'You mean . . .' Sara couldn't say it.

'I mean that both your parents sought love in other places besides the conjugal bed. They were devoted to you, but even that tie frazzled under the stress of the marriage. Bill and Marion were too similar; they were both explosive and impulsive. Believe me, Sara, they're far better off apart than together.'

Sara sat and stared into the dregs of her coffee. Of course, she'd known how mismatched her parents were. They both had tempers that lit immediately and could flare out of control. She knew very well that part of her own calm and mastery of her emotions came from a very early desire not to be like her parents, not to allow anger to cloud her judgment, not to be caught in the screaming battles that were fought with greater and greater frequency during her childhood.

'Elissa told me about Dad and Miss Dukes,' she said in a low voice.

Betty saw the pain on her face. 'Don't blame him, Sara. Your mother probably locked him out of the bedroom, and he was a man who needed love and affection.'

But I was there, Sara wanted to say, the child in her rushing to the surface. He had me! She was old enough to know now that a daughter was no compensation in a man's life for lack of a woman, and she even suspected that without Miss Dukes, her father might have left them long before she was a teenager, but the knowledge still cut deep as if she had old wounds not yet completely healed. 'We never really grow up, do we?' she asked with a sigh, and Betty, instead of being confused by the non sequitur, understood it perfectly.

'You'll always have strong feelings about your parents,' she replied soothingly. 'You can't forget the past. If you're still angry and upset about the divorce, then acknowledge it. Don't bury the feelings and allow them to eat away at you.'

Echoes of Lee and Elissa. 'I've always felt that Dad abandoned me,' Sara confessed.

Betty leaned back, her fingers gently scratching the ears of the cat on her lap. 'Why?'

'Because he went to California.'

'And got married and had more children.'

Sara gave her aunt a rueful look. 'I know, I'm jealous.'

Betty shrugged. 'It's natural, I'd say, but you have to see it from his perspective. The California job was far too good for him to pass up and he'd always hated the commuting into New York. I know he didn't want to leave you, but he had his own life to lead and by then you were already sixteen and very close to leaving home yourself.'

'I don't see him very often.'

'Now, Sara, whose choice is that?'

Sara was stung. 'He never writes, every once in a while he phones . . .'

'Sheba! Watch those claws. Damn thing should be declawed and defanged. She's ruined more skirts of mine.' Betty shifted the cat in her lap.

'All right,' Sara admitted reluctantly. 'Maybe some of it's been my fault.'

'Bill says the same things: that you don't write or phone.'

It would be hard for Sara to explain to anyone how she felt about her father's new family. She'd visited them once, the year she was twenty-one, and she'd felt like a complete outsider, although it was no one's fault but her own. Her father's new wife, Danielle, had gone out of her way to make her feel at home, and her twin half-brothers, aged three then, had been delighted to have a newly discovered sister, but they had all been so carefree and so happy together that Sara had felt like an appendage. Her father was a different man than the one she had known; he'd been tanned, relaxed and smiling all the time, and she envied his second family the father his first had never had.

'Perhaps I should try more,' she acknowledged.

'Not a bad idea. Pour me another cup, will you? And what about your mother? She doesn't see much of you either.'

Sara filled the proffered mug. 'The prodigal daughter?' she asked.

'I'm not the person you should be talking to, Sara. If you have questions about the past then go to the source. Talk to Marion; she'll tell you what you want to know.'

Sara shook her head. 'We've never been close.'

'Come now! You were always siding with your father and you never gave Marion half a chance. I think you'd be surprised at how she would welcome your interest.'

Sara thought of her fastidious mother. 'She'd hate raking up old coals.'

Betty took a deep swig of coffee and gave her a look tht was both severe and chastising. 'Maybe she'd do it for you. Have you thought of that?'

Sara took the train back to Manhattan after spending the afternoon walking the beach with her aunt. It had been cool but sunny, the waters of the Sound quiet and placid, its surface reflecting the sun in a sparkling, random pattern. Gulls had wheeled over their heads, and the hardy clam diggers had been out on their rigs, plying their enormous shovels deep into the murky bottom of the inlet. In the distance, Sara could see the far shore of Connecticut as a dark green finger lying across the horizon, and she remembered her childhood ambition to swim the seven miles distance. All the children had wanted to do it then; they'd even once spent the weekend huddled in a nearby tree-house planning the excursion, excited by news of English Channel swimmers.

The smell of salt and low tide had brought on a flood of reminiscences, and Sara and her aunt had talked and laughed about events that had occurred ten years before. They talked about Elissa most of all, remembering her as a troublemaker and hell-raiser and shaking their heads over her transformation into a dedicated musician. Betty confessed that she was just as shocked at Elissa's devotion as Sara. 'I never thought I'd see the day that child would settle down. She was the most restless thing in jeans this side of the Mississippi.'

'She's very talented,' Sara reminded her.

'Don't know where it comes from,' Betty had said. 'I have a tin ear and her father couldn't hold a tune to save his life.'

Sara thought about the ways people could change as she rode home on the train and arrived back at her apartment, wondering if Betty's suggestion about talking to her mother was really worthwhile. Try as she might, Sara couldn't imagine having a decent conversation with Marion. They'd never been able to talk and since her remarriage, their communication had almost come to a standstill. Sara had always blamed her mother for being so impossible and rigid, but now she suspected that she might have been part of the problem. She *had* favoured her father, but she had never guessed that Marion had been jealous or that he had come between them so effectively that her mother had given up trying to reach her. Even after the divorce and right up to the time he had left for California, Sara had spent as much time with him as possible, cooking meals for him in his tiny apartment and trying hard, in her adolescent way, to play the role of a wife. She had been bereft when he moved and she had accused her mother of forcing him to leave. That had been a fight of gargantuan proportions, and she shuddered even to remember it.

Marion's marriage after Sara had moved to Manhattan had come as a tremendous relief. As cool as the feelings were between them, Sara had had feelings of responsibility to her mother, especially after she had gone and Marion had been left alone in that big house, but her new stepfather had taken the burden of worrying off her shoulders. Gregory Stonehauser, a widower and retired Army general, had met her mother at a party, swept her off her feet, married her in two months and moved her down to Washington where he still consulted for the Army. It had all happened very quickly and very satisfactorily. Sara had visited them once, noted that her mother seemed happy and flown back to Manhattan, feeling for the first time that she was truly free.

There were two phone messages when she got back; one was from Lee and the other was from Peter. Sara looked at them and had the intense desire to tear both up. She felt too raw from the things her aunt had told her to face Lee, and she knew Peter was going to be difficult. They were heading for some sort of confrontation and Sara shrank from it. She liked Peter and she was going to hurt him. She saw no other way of ending what should never have started in the first place. She blamed herself for letting their relationship get to the point where Peter could get jealous over another man; she should have told Peter months ago that she didn't love him, but she'd been a coward then and she wasn't much braver now. Sara stared at his name, scribbled in Elissa's rounded handwriting, and had the urge to crawl into bed and bury her head under the covers.

She called Lee first.

'How are you?' he said, his voice deep over the telephone.

'I'm fine,' she said coolly. She wasn't about to tell him that she had visited her aunt to talk about the past. She needed time to digest what she had learned without interference.

'I'm not,' he said. 'I'm dripping on to the carpet. You got me out of the shower.'

'Oh,' was all Sara could manage. Her mouth went dry at the thought of Lee standing there in the nude. She had seen him half-naked on the screen and knew just how perfect his body was. His lean, muscular physique was part of his sensual charisma. Fan magazines always pictured him in a bathing suit, and one glossy magazine that had just done an interview with him had taken photos of him lounging in his California home, in jeans and bare to the waist, his wide chest dark with hair.

It seemed Lee could read her mind, even across Manhattan. 'Does it turn you on?' he asked in low voice.

Sara cleared her throat. 'Don't be ridiculous!'

'Mmmm, it does, I can tell.' Lee gave a soft laugh. 'Why don't I give you a description. Do you want it from the head down or the toes up?'

'I'm going to hang up,' she threatened.

'Sorry, I forgot that you're the lady who doesn't like to talk about sex.'

'Sexual innuendoes,' she corrected him.

'You mean hints that there's more to life than work?'

Sara's dander was beginning to rise. 'If you wanted me to answer your call, just so that you could insult . . .'

'Whoa!' he exclaimed, laughing. 'Come to a dinner party with me on Saturday night. I want you to meet some friends of mine.'

'I don't . . .'

'Don't refuse. It's impolite.'

'I've been thinking about what you said and I don't . . .'

'Thinking is dangerous for your health, and if you say no, I'll start sending you roses again.'

She couldn't help smiling. 'You're not playing fair,' she said. 'You know I don't have enough vases.'

'I'll send you an entire florist's shop,' he warned.

'Lee, I . . .'

'Great. I'll pick you up at eight.'

He had hung up before she could answer, and Sara ruefully admitted to herself that she hadn't wanted to say no in the first place. Even talking to Lee on the telephone made her tense with an excitement that she couldn't deny. It was almost as if she was becoming addicted to him and that flare of sensuality he inspired in her. She wanted to be with him, even when she knew that he wasn't good for her. Like a junkie, she craved that jolt of sexual intensity.

Rather than think about it, she called Peter, and to her surprise, he was cheerful and buoyant. He'd been apartment-hunting and found three places he wanted her to see with him, saying that he wasn't much good at judging a kitchen. Sara, thankful for his good mood, agreed and met him after a quick dinner. The first apartment they saw was impossible in her opinion; despite its location near the bank where Peter worked, the rooms were cramped and the plumbing dated from the turn of the century. The second apartment was a loft that would require complete renovation, and Peter agreed that he probably wasn't up to the task. The third, however, was charming and had real potential if he didn't mind painting. It had one large bedroom and one small closet-like room that could be an office. The kitchen was narrow but well designed and the living room had an expanse of glass wall with a panoramic view of the city skyline.

'I like this one,' said Sara after she had walked through the empty rooms, her footsteps echoing against the walls. 'Even the floors are nice.'

They both stared down at the wooden floors, polished to a high sheen. 'It's been well kept,' Peter commented.

'Mmm.' Sara walked around the living room, trying to judge its size in comparison to Peter's furniture. He didn't have much, but what he did have was of fairly good quality. She had always given him credit for at least trying to decorate and not sinking to the depths of orange crates and brick bookshelves. 'The couch could go here,' she said with enthusiasm. 'And your table could sit in this corner.'

Peter smiled, his blue eyes lighting up at the tone of her voice. 'I might buy a breakfront,' he said.

'Good idea!' she agreed. 'There aren't that many kitchen cabinets to hold your china.'

'Sara . . .' Peter stepped forward, but just at that second the building superintendent walked in through the opened front door.

'Made up your mind, folks?' he asked. He was a rotund little man with a balding head of hair and a thick, greying moustache, who looked from Peter to his well-tailored slacks and camel wool coat to Sara, dressed in an obviously expensive beige silk dress, and sized them up, not quite accurately. 'I don't really have to give you a sales spiel on this place. I've got people lined up to see it, but it's a great place for a young couple. Good for entertaining and lots of space for expansion.' He winked at Peter. 'The master bedroom's big enough for a king-size bed and the second bedroom would make a dandy room for a baby. And it's close enough to the elevator so you don't have to traipse so far with the groceries.'

Sara cleared her throat. 'I'm afraid . . .'

'As I said, I've got another couple waiting. I don't want to push you folks, but good apartments are hard to come by in this city.' He looked at them expectantly.

'We'll take it,' said Peter.

'Good. Come on down to the office and you two can sign the lease.' He gave them a welcoming smile. 'It'll be a pleasure to have you in the building, Mr and Mrs Gray.'

Peter had thought it funny, but Sara wasn't amused at all. The superintendent mistaking them for a married couple was far too close to what might have happened to her if she'd allowed herself to drift along, falling slowly but surely into Peter's plans for her future. Lee had changed all that; he had jolted her into an awareness of herself that hadn't existed before. She had always known that Peter wasn't the right man for her, but she hadn't actually understood why, and without that ability to articulate her feelings, Sara had followed Peter's lead; dating him, making meals for him and, by her silence, giving credibility to his dreams for the future.

After Peter had signed the lease and put down his security deposit, they went to a nearby restaurant for dessert and coffee. It was a cosy place, almost empty at that time of night, with tables tucked behind ferns and decorated with red-checked cloths and bright red napkins. Peter pulled out the chair for her, gave the waiter an exuberant smile and ordered them both large slices of Brandy Alexander Pie.

'My waistline!' Sara protested.

'We're celebrating,' he said happily. 'We just rented our apartment.'

'*Your* apartment,' she corrected him, her heart sinking as she recognised the path his thoughts were taking.

He leaned forward and took her hand. 'Sara, it might be a little premature, but now that I've taken the place—well, it seems ridiculous not to say it. You know that I want to marry you and the apartment is perfect for a couple. I don't see why we couldn't move in together.'

'Peter . . .'

'I know it means giving up your place, but this one is bigger. It's got an extra bathroom and . . .'

Sara tried to stem the rush of words. She pulled her hand away. 'Peter, I'm not ready to marry anyone.'

His blue eyes were unhappy. 'It's a big step,' he admitted, 'and I know that my first marriage was a failure, but you're not anything like Karen. It would be different for us.'

She sighed. 'It has nothing to do with your first marriage.'

'Move in with me then. I'd rather marry you, but if you're afraid, we can try living together.'

Sara's eyes widened at the thought. 'Oh, no!' she protested. 'I couldn't do that.'

Peter was immediately contrite, wrongly imagining that her horrified response arose from outraged morals instead of distaste. 'I'm sorry I mentioned it. Please forgive me. You're not that sort of a woman.'

'I don't know how to say this,' she began, looking unhappily at Peter's face and noting how boyish he looked with his brown hair falling on to his forehead and his blue eyes pleading and expectant, 'but I don't think we should have ever started dating in the first place.'

'What do you mean?'

This time it was Sara who leaned forward, her face earnest. 'We're not right for one another. We're too similar.'

'In what way?'

'We're both quiet and introverted and ... subdued. We'd get bored with one another in a year. I know we would.'

'I'm sorry you feel that way,' he said stiffly. 'I don't think I'd ever get bored with you.'

'Why couldn't he see it? You would, Peter. You'd spend evenings staring at me and eventually you'd wonder if there wasn't something else to do.'

'I thought we'd have children. I always wanted kids, but Karen didn't.'

Sara looked down at her clenched hands. 'I'm sorry,' she said in a low voice.

There was a long silence and then Peter spoke again, his voice bitter. 'Why the hell did you let me rent that apartment? I did it for you.'

'Please,' she begged him, 'don't say that. You did it for yourself. You need a nicer place to live.'

'Sara!' He took her wrist this time and wouldn't let go. 'I love you. For God's sake, don't you understand that?'

She was thankful that they were in a secluded corner and that the tables around them were empty. 'Not love,' she said, shaking her head. 'There's no ... passion between us.'

'Passion!' He spat the word out of his mouth as if it had a foul taste. 'I had passion with Karen and it went nowhere. Passion's no good if there's no compatibility.'

His grip was so tight he was hurting her wrist, but Sara aimed for a reasonable tone. 'And compatibility's no good by itself either. We're friends, Peter. Nothing more than friends.'

He was about to speak again, when the waiter came by, looking tired and bored and announcing that the restaurant would be closing soon. Peter let go of her wrist and Sara surreptitiously rubbed it to get the circulation moving again. They didn't speak any more but picked at their food and then left, Peter insisting that he pay the bill when Sara tried to take her wallet out of her purse.

They walked in silence for a few blocks and Sara, rather than look at Peter, watched the rush of traffic, the taxis zig-zagging through the streets, their horns blaring. Even on a Sunday night, the city streets were clogged with cars and the sidewalks held groups of people rushing in different directions. The hustle and bustle had a way of making Sara's mind go into neutral, as if the noise drove out all thought from her head. She enjoyed the mindless walking, wanting to forget the man beside her whose back was curved with un-happiness, his fists jammed into his coat pockets. Sara hoped against hope that she'd make it back to the apartment without any further discussion, but Peter evidently had another course of action in mind. When they turned on to a quiet side street, he began again.

'Sara, why don't we try to go away together? Perhaps, if we got away from New York for a week or so, spent some time with one another, and concentrated on our relationship. I'm busy and you're so wound up with B.J. and your play . . .'

Sara sighed. 'It wouldn't work.'

He stopped on a dark corner, took her by the shoulder and pushed her next to a building and away from a few passersby. 'Why not?'

'Because we're not right for one another, because . . .'

'Because you don't love me. That's what you're really trying to say.' There was anger in his voice, and Sara remembered her earlier fear that Peter was capable of great fury when he was aroused. Certainly, she could feel the strength of his fingers even through the thickness of her wool coat.

'I wish I did,' she said with a note of desperation in her voice. 'You don't know how much I've wanted to love you. I've . . . tried.'

'So what's stopping you now?'

'I just realised that . . .'

'It's that movie star, isn't it?'

'Don't be crazy. He has nothing to do with it.'

'Doesn't he?'

Sara looked up into Peter's face and suddenly noticed how harsh and forbidding he looked in the gleam of a street light. His eyes were deep, dark wells and his mouth was a severe, straight line. 'I've known for a long time,' she said hastily, 'that I didn't love you.'

'I wonder,' he said coldly.

'Lee doesn't count,' she said.

'So it's *Lee*, is it? That sounds . . . intimate.'

'We're not intimate,' Sara protested.

'Has he kissed you?'

'Peter! I . . .'

'So he has.' There was a dead quality to Peter's voice. 'You're a fool to think he'd be interested in you.'

It hurt to hear Peter say it even though in her heart of hearts she agreed. 'I . . . know I would be. He has lots of women; he doesn't need me.'

'Do you enjoy his kisses more than mine?'

'This is a silly conversation.' Sara tried to turn away and start walking, but Peter wouldn't let her go, his hand moving down her arm in a tight grasp.

'I asked you a question,' he said, and she could tell that his teeth were clenched together.

'Don't do it,' she begged him, guessing with horror what was coming. 'People are watching.'

Peter ignored her and anyone else on the street.

'Maybe I should have tried harder,' he grated. 'Like this.'

He had kissed her before, but he had always touched her with a gentleness that she thought was intrinsic to his nature. Sara had never suspected that there was this other side of him; a side that could be furious and hard and violent. He took her mouth so harshly that her bottom lip grated against her teeth and she tasted blood. He tried to rouse her, his fingers pulling open the buttons of her coat so that he could reach in and touch her breast through the fabric of her dress. The other hand cupped the back of her head, his fingers tangling in her hair. Through it all, Sara stood silent and passive, knowing that he had to take his anger out somehow and suspecting that, when it was all over, he was going to feel ashamed and humilated.

Finally, to her utter relief, Peter lifted his head, took his hand off her breast and stepped away from her. 'Damn,' he muttered. 'God damn!'

'Peter,' she put her hand out and tentatively touched his arm, 'don't blame yourself. It's my fault. You're a good man and you deserve someone better than me.'

'He's going to use you,' Peter said. 'Don't say I haven't warned you.'

'I know what he's like,' she said defensively.

'But you're still going out with him, aren't you?'

She was about to deny it, but her phone call with Lee came back to mind and she hesitated.

'What kind of future do you have with a man like that? We could have made a family, had children and a life together. Lee Cameron isn't going to give you anything but heartbreak.'

'I know that,' she said.

'Then why do you see him?'

'He's in the play and . . .'

'He's sexy.'

Sara couldn't deny it; Lee was the sexiest man she'd ever met. 'Yes,' she whispered.

Peter went on relentlessly. 'He cultivates it. He makes his money turning women on.'

'I know,' she said miserably.

'You're in love with him, aren't you?'

She shook her head. 'No.'

'I don't believe you.'

'It's . . . just an infatuation.'

'You're a stupid fool, Sara, to fall in love with a man who'll drop you tomorrow for a pretty face,' snapped Peter, slamming his fist into his hand in a gesture of utter frustration. 'A stupid fool!'

CHAPTER SEVEN

LOVE . . . What Sara thought she knew about love could have been written on the head of a pin. She had never been exposed to very much of it, at least not the sort that occurs between a man and a woman. Her parents' marriage was based on dislike and her aunt had been widowed when she was too young to remember much about it. No, Sara decided after she had returned home that night, what she knew about was the aftermath of love, the wreckage that occurs when passion or love crashes on the rocks of incompatibility.

The result was that she didn't know what she felt about Lee. She was more inclined to believe that what had hit her was lust at first sight, rather than love. The physical attraction was awesome, an invisible connection that sprang to life the moment she thought about him, talked to him on the telephone or saw him. She had never before been subjected to the sensations that overcame her at the mere mention of his name. They made her feel alternately giddy, weak, hot, cold and breathless. It was like a sickness, she concluded, an illness that had no cure . . . except satiation, and Sara knew that she wasn't ready for that. She didn't believe in casual affairs or one-night stands. She had enough self-knowledge to know the pitfalls of leaping into bed with a man for the sake of satisfying a sexual yen. She'd be wretched afterwards, her sense of integrity and dignity broken under a yoke of shame.

Which left her nowhere to go except into the depths of frustration, and she was rapidly learning how unpleasant they were. Her appetite suffered and her sleep was broken by restless dreams and constant wakings. She couldn't concentrate on her work and B.J., who had already chided her for daydreaming, now let her have it, broadside on.

'If I'd wanted an idiot running this office,' he said one afternoon when Sara couldn't find the letter she'd just typed, 'I'd have hired one.'

'I can't imagine what happened to it. It isn't like me to lose things. I don't know . . .'

B.J. leaned back in his big chair and transfixed her with a keen, blue-eyed stare. 'You're sighing into the coffee. You can't keep your mind on two things at once, and damned if I didn't find the Marchello folder in the fridge.'

'In the fridge!' Sara couldn't believe her ears. They kept a small refrigerator and stove in a room beside B.J.'s office. It was handy for making meals, particularly when the office went into overtime.

'Next to the mayonnaise,' he growled.

Sara sat down abruptly in the chair opposite his desk. 'I'm sorry, B.J., really I am.'

'Is it the play or Lee Cameron?'

'I haven't been sleeping well and . . .'

'Don't evade the question,' he said curtly.

'A bit of both,' she confessed.

'The play's going well. It's going to be a smash; we've got a great cast.' B.J. pulled a cigar out of a box on his desk and lit it with a flourish of satisfaction. 'A hit.'

'That will be nice,' she said dully.

'And you've got a crush on the leading man.'

'Lee and I have been . . . dating,' she said carefully.

His fierce white eyebrows raised a notch. 'That's a genteel way of putting it,' he commented.

'I'm not having an affair with him!'

He studied her down-turned face. 'Maybe that's the problem. Why don't you and get it out of your system?'

'B.J.! I don't believe in . . .'

He waved his cigar at her. 'Are you one of those

females who holds out for marriage?' he asked in distaste.

Sara flushed even pinker than she had before. 'It's Lee,' she explained. 'He has women falling all over him.'

'And you don't want to join the crowd?'

She shook her head. 'It would be humiliating.'

'Hmm.' For a second, a fleeting glance of sympathy passed over B.J.'s face and was immediately followed by a scowl. 'Well, do as you damn please, but get your head in order. Your efficiency's gone to hell.'

Sara stood up, knowing that she was excused. 'I'll try,' she said.

'And find that letter.'

'Yes, sir.' She walked to the door.

'And keep our business files out of the mayonnaise.'

'Aye, aye, sir.'

'And, Sara?'

She turned. 'Yes?'

'Keep your chin up, baby. You've got some tough times ahead.'

Sara hadn't known just how tough resisting Lee could be until he began phoning her every night. The calls seemed innocuous. He refrained from sexual comments, talking about rehearsals and asking how her day had gone. She found herself looking forward to his calls, and the one night that Sara didn't hear from him, she was restless and unhappy, finally throwing herself into a rampage of cleaning closets to keep her mind off the silent telephone.

Peter's words echoed in her mind with an ever-increasing intensity. Lee was everything Peter had called him; a celebrity who made his career out of displaying his sexual charisma. He had no particular need for Sara; he could have almost any woman at the snap of his fingers, and the fact that he was obviously trying to forge some sort of connection between them, sexual or otherwise, made her increasingly suspicious. She racked her brains to understand why Lee was pursuing her and could come up with only one explanation that fitted the circumstances. Like any artist, Lee wanted to create the perfect masterpiece. As a writer, Sara knew how shamelessly she listened to overheard conversations and encouraged the confidences of friends and acquaintances to find material for her work. Lee was being no different. He wanted *Adjustments* to be a success, and what better way was there to understand the play than to cultivate the playwright and pick her brains?

The fact that the playwright was a woman who was reasonably pretty and unattached was simply the icing on the cake. Sara knew that Lee was attracted to her; their sensual bond was mutual, but she realised that his emotions went no deeper than those suitable to a profitable liaison for the play's run. She was being used; Peter was right, but the problem was that Sara, caught in the web of Lee's charm and virile magnetism, was a willing victim. She couldn't deny that she liked hearing from him. When she picked up the receiver and heard his low and masculine voice at the other end, she felt a glow of heady anticipation. He wasn't always solemn and serious; sometimes he flirted with her, although always in a lighthearted and teasing manner. They discovered through these phone calls a mutual interest in modern art, French writers and opera. Lee rarely mentioned Sara's concerns about the play, and Sara gave him points for smart tactics. The sort of probing Lee was after required sensitivity, and she knew he was handling her with kid gloves.

But she couldn't summon anger at his manipulations. She was far too deep into that rush of adrenalin, that instant warmth that hit her at the sound of his voice. She knew that their date for dinner held a potential danger, but she looked forward to it all the same and dressed for it with special care, leaving her red hair hanging loose to her bare shoulders and wearing a dress of flowing blue and green chiffon whose bodice was held up by the slenderest of straps. She put silver hoops in her ears and a silver chain around her neck; the outfit completed by silvery high-heeled sandals and a tiny silver purse. Sara swirled in front of the mirror, nodded approvingly to her image and, with a tension brought on by days of anticipation, met Lee in the lobby of her building.

He didn't disappoint her. 'You look lovely,' he said, taking her hand and bringing it up to his mouth, his dark head bent over her wrist.

Sara shivered at his kiss on her palm, but acted nonchalant. 'Straight out of *The Pirate's Sword*,' she said tartly, pulling her hand out of his grasp.

'I didn't know you'd seen my B movies,' Lee said ruefully.

'They show the re-runs on late-night television.'

He grimaced and then laughed. 'I have a feeling, Sara, that you know just how to cut me down to size.'

They took a taxi to an address on Central Park and Lee ushered her into a luxurious apartment where the door was answered by a maid in a black uniform, and Sara was offered a drink by a waiter who was carrying chilled goblets of white and red wine on a wide silver tray. The room was breathtakingly large and decorated with no thought to expense. Sara caught sight of panoramic windows edged with long velvet curtains of a dark hunter's green, oil paintings on the wall, and a richly patterned Persian carpet with long white fringes on the gleaming oaken floors. She was just about to comment on how beautiful the room was when a woman dressed in an elegant silk caftan of ivory and blue came up to Lee and threw her arms around him. She was attractive and in her late forties, Sara judged, her dark chignon streaked with grey, laughter lines wrinkling the skin around her eyes.

'Lee! It's wonderful to see you!' She pushed him away slightly and gave him a disapproving look from her fine dark eyes. 'You don't come to New York often enough.'

He smiled at her. 'And you, Fiona, have been gallivanting around Europe or you'd know that I've been here two months already rehearsing.'

'I know everything that you're up to,' she said scoldingly, then turned with a warm smile. 'And this must be Sara.'

'The playwright who wrote all the lines I've been memorising,' Lee agreed, introducing them. 'Sara, this is Fiona Kerne. She and her husband, Dave, fed and housed me when I was an out-of-work actor with empty pockets and no prospects.'

Fiona tucked her arm through Sara's. 'Don't listen to him,' she confided teasingly. 'Hollywood ate him up almost the moment he arrived. The truth was that he was shy and lonely, and Dave and I acted like surrogate parents.'

Sara threw a quick glance at Lee, trying to imagine him as shy and lonely and then giving up. He was tall and handsome in a well-tailored grey suit that set off his dark good looks and muscular physique, not hiding the width of his shoulders, the taut lines of his waist and hips or the long length of his legs. He had an aura of confidence that ran so deep that she couldn't envisage him any other way.

Fiona noticed her expression. 'It's hard to believe,' she said with a smile, 'but Lee was once a hick from the sticks who didn't know an hors d'oeuvre from an aperitif. Come, let me introduce you to the others.'

The people who had gathered for dinner that night in Fiona's apartment were all friends of long standing who shared a companionable warmth and easy laughter.

Fiona and Dave were the oldest, a handsome couple, both tall, dark-haired and distinguished and, Sara guessed from the conversation, independently wealthy. There was another married couple, the Aberdeens, who were involved somehow with television, Bert McHenry who was a movie critic for a New York paper and the Kernes' daughter, Marcie, a pretty girl of about sixteen who had an obvious crush on Lee.

For dinner they sat around a long mahogany table under a chandelier whose lights had been turned down until they cast a golden glow over the cutlery and the cobalt blue rim of the bone china. The meal was served by two waiters, a crown roast of lamb, wild rice, and a salad of avocados and hearts of palm. The elegance of it all didn't seem to subdue anyone but Sara. The conversation was animated, lively and filled with bursts of laughter. Lee's latest movie was teasingly lambasted by all at the table except for Marcie, who had loved it and insisted that it was his best.

'Could you be prejudiced?' John Aberdeen asked indulgently.

Marcie shook her head, her french braid of brown hair swinging on her neck. 'Lee was great in it. He was so . . . so . . .'

'Macho?' he asked drily.

'But nice,' she insisted. 'When you saved the girl, you were so sweet to her.'

Lee gave her a grin. 'Spoken like a true fan!'

'Marcie's one of your best,' Dave agreed. 'She's seen all your films at least five times.'

'Not like Sara,' said Lee, glancing at her wryly. 'She doesn't like them.'

Bert, who was sitting opposite Sara, leaned forward, his round face looking suitably impressed. 'Speak,' he commanded. 'I always need new material for my column.'

Sara gave him a smile. 'I don't like thrillers,' she said.

'Hear, hear,' said Joan Aberdeen, a well-groomed, elegant blonde. 'Neither do I.'

The conversation turned to taste in entertainment and went on to the Broadway stage and the current crop of plays. The group were curious about *Adjustments*, but Sara found it easier to channel the discussion to Lee. She wasn't quite capable of talking about her play in public. As he talked, she saw that he belonged to this kind of the people, the type whose wealth or background gave them so much self-confidence that they were his equals. She, on the other hand, couldn't help feeling shy, despite their obvious interest in her as a playwright. They were wealthy, influential and articulate and she was none of those things. Peter had said that she'd be a fool to fall for Lee, and Sara could see that he was right. She didn't fit in with such a sparkling crowd; she had nothing to commend herself, not beauty or money or witty conversation. The knowledge didn't make Sara feel sorry for herself; she had always known her particular niche in society, but it did reaffirm the feeling that she and Lee moved in separate worlds whose elements, like oil and water, didn't mix well.

After dinner, when dessert and coffee were served in the living room, Sara found herself sitting next to Fiona on a loveseat. The older woman, who seemed to sense that Sara's restraint came from shyness, drew her out about B.J. and her job, remarking that she thought Sara had a very exciting career.

'Not really,' Sara said. 'Merely hectic.'

'You don't enjoy working with stars.'

'Some are better than others.'

Fiona gave her an odd look. 'Like Lee?'

Of course, Sara had known it was coming. She'd seen the curious looks that the Kernes had thrown her way, and knew that they were questioning what Lee saw in her. They teased him, but it was obvious that they were very fond of him, and she couldn't blame them for wondering or being concerned. He was like a son to them and treated Marcie like a younger sister.

'Lee has less arrogance than most,' Sara said cautiously.

'How serious is this?' Fiona asked gently.

Sara put off answering. 'Serious?' she asked.

'Whatever's between you and Lee.'

'Not serious at all,' Sara assured her.

'You must think I'm interfering where I don't belong, but you're the first woman Lee's ever introduced us to.'

Sara looked at her in wide-eyed astonishment.

Fiona nodded. 'We've had him to dinner many times, but he's always come alone.'

'I would have thought . . .' Sara began, then her voice trailed away.

'Lee's far more fastidious about women than the gossip columns would allow,' Fiona said. 'He's had a few; he's far from being a saint, but they've all been unimportant as far as I know.'

Sara gave a poor imitation of a nonchalant shrug. 'I'm sure I'm nothing more than that,' she said. 'The play is our connection.'

Fiona gave her a smile. 'You think that's all?'

'What else could it be? I hardly qualify otherwise.'

'Perhaps you underestimate yourself.'

'I don't think so,' Sara said firmly. 'I'm not beautiful or glamorous. Lee can have his pick of women like that.'

'But when he looks at you, Sara, there's something in his eyes that I've never seen before.'

'Frustration,' Sara said lightly. 'We're always arguing about the play.'

Fiona shook her head and put her hand gently on Sara's arm. 'Do me a favour?' she asked.

'Of course,' Sara replied.

'Don't hurt him. He's far more vulnerable than you think.'

Sara stared at her in surprise and then towards Lee, who was standing by the fireplace talking to Bert, his elbow resting on the mantelpiece, one hand in the pocket of his slacks, his jacket unbuttoned to reveal a white shirt moulded to his flat abdomen. The light from a lamp turned his hair to a gleaming black and emphasised the bronze quality of his skin and the hard planes of his face. He hardly looked vulnerable, Sara thought; he looked invincible, as if nothing could ever touch him, much less hurt him.

'He may not seem that way,' Fiona said softly as if she could read Sara's mind, 'but believe me, he is. Lee's developed a tough façade to survive, but there's more to the man than his exterior. If you have his heart, Sara, you hold his life in your hands.'

Lee's heart, Sara decided much later, was quite free and untrammeled despite Fiona's words. He'd taken her home after the party in a taxi, kissed her without demand and said goodbye. If those were the actions of a man in love then Sara didn't have a clue what made the male of the species click. She'd been prepared for every eventuality; Lee enticing her to his apartment or following her up to hers or, even worse, starting to make love to her in the taxi. Instead, he had put his arm around her and pulled her close to him, but that had been the extent of their physical contact. If he'd guessed that Sara wanted more, he hadn't shown an inkling of it.

'Thank you for coming,' he had said when the taxi pulled up before her apartment building.

'I enjoyed your friends,' she told him.

'I think they liked you. I saw that Fiona had you in a huddle.'

'She's very fond of you.'

Lee had raised a dark eyebrow. 'Talking about me?'

'Fiona wanted to make sure that I'd take care of your ego.'

He had put his head back and laughed. 'Fiona's a mother hen—she's been worried about me for years.' He looked at her. 'And will you?'

'Will I what?'

'Take care of my ego.'

'Of course not,' Sara had said tartly. 'It's already too big as it is.'

'I knew you'd say that.' And that was when he had leaned forward and brushed his mouth gently against hers. 'Goodnight, Sara. I'll call you tomorrow.'

The end result was that Sara, keyed up to either fighting him off or being overwhelmed by his advances, felt empty and deflated, wondering with a rueful feeling if she shouldn't begin a regimen of cold showers. She had longed to touch him as they sat next to one another, the taxi racing through the city streets, bars of light and shadow alternately illuminating his face and then throwing it into darkness. She had yearned to caress the lean line of his cheek and tangle her fingers through the dark strands of his hair. She wanted him, and Sara could feel that wanting so badly she could almost taste it. She wanted to sleep with him, she finally admitted to herself with a feeling of surrender. She wanted to lie beside him on a bed and feel his skin against hers. She wanted to touch his chest with the palms of her hands and trace the line of his body hair over his muscled stomach until . . .

'Scrambled or sunny side up? Sara! Are you listening? I've asked you twice already.'

Sara came out of her reverie to find herself in the kitchen, dressed in her bathrobe, with Elissa standing opposite her, her hands on her hips, her head shaking in disapproval. She gave Elissa a shaky smile. 'Sorry—I was thinking.'

'About what? You were miles away.'

Sara shrugged. 'Nothing much.'

Elissa, who was dressed in a blue-sprigged cotton nightgown propped herself up on a stool, entwined her slippered foot through the bottom rung and gave Sara an inquisitorial look. 'Come on now, spill the beans to cousin Elissa!'

'Just a few problems,' Sara said casually. 'Nothing of import.'

'Is it Peter?'

'We're not going out any more.'

'I know; he told me.'

'He did?'

Elissa nodded and picked up a piece of toast. 'Cried on my shoulder, to be precise. I should have been wearing a wet suit; the guy is really broken up about it.'

'He asked me to marry him and I had to tell him no.' Sara gave her cousin a beseeching look. 'It's for the best. We would have bored each other to death.'

'He's waiting for you to come to your senses.'

'Our breaking up has nothing to do with Lee.'

Elissa gave her an appraising look as she took a bite of toast. 'No?' she asked.

Emphatically, 'No!'

'Hmm. Well, that's good, because your leading man seems to be developing a romantic attachment elsewhere.'

Sara felt her face turn hot and she quickly looked away from Elissa. She'd known; deep inside, she'd known that there had to be another woman. Lee hadn't touched her last night. He'd treated her with affection as if she were a friend, not a prospective lover. Of course there was another woman. Someone who was lovely and elegant; someone who could spark his interest.

'It's all in there,' said Elissa, pointing to the Sunday newspaper. 'Now, will it be scrambled eggs or sunny side up?'

Sara stood up, casually tucking the paper under her arm. 'Neither,' she said. 'I'm not very hungry.'

'But you said earlier that you were starving.'

'I've ... changed my mind. I think I'll lie down for a while.'

Elissa gave her a curious glance. 'This thing with Lee is getting to you, isn't it?'

'Of course not,' Sara snapped. 'I couldn't care less.'

'Right,' Elissa said smartly, jumping off the stool and heading towards the stove. 'You don't give a damn.'

'Exactly,' replied Sara with vehemence as she headed out the door. 'Lee Cameron could drop dead and I wouldn't give a tinker's damn!'

Her hands trembled and the pages of the newspaper rattled between her fingers. The gossip column seemed to be lost somewhere between the finance and the sports sections, and Sara thought she would never find it, but when she did, she wished she hadn't. The story sprang at her in pictorial splendor. There was a photograph of Lee in a tuxedo getting out of a taxi with his arm around a smiling blonde dressed in an evening gown. She wasn't quite as Sara had imagined her to be. She was neither voluptuous nor beautiful nor wealthy, but then she didn't have to be. Felicia had more talent than most people combined and was more clever and funny than a barrel full of monkeys. Lee had often talked about her with admiration. There was no reason why Sara should be surprised. Wasn't it logical that her leading man would fall in love with one of his leading ladies?

Certainly the reporter thought so, and had waxed poetic about a liaison between the stars of a Broadway show. The adjectives flowed in abundance: charming, delightful, fey and gamine were used to describe Felicia; Lee was breathlessly hailed as sexy, gorgeous, raven-haired and thrilling, but then the reporter was female and Sara could forgive her the superlatives. She knew the effect that Lee had on women.

The article went on to describe Lee and Felicia's arrival at an opening night, a post-show dinner and then a short side trip to a night club. The reporter had followed the cab home and seen both occupants leave the taxi for Lee's hotel. She speculated on their ensuing behaviour, her language just short of libellous, and made suggestive comments about their stunning future together as Broadway lovers. Sara, however, had lost interest in the spicy details. She had noticed, almost immediately, that Lee and Felicia's night out corresponded with the one night that Lee hadn't phoned her, and it hurt to think he had been trying to seduce her by phone while he was planning a romantic evening with Felicia.

Then Sara sat back against her pillow and, taking a deep breath, chided herself for believing everything that she read. She knew how the newspapers exaggerated, and everyone in the entertainment business knew how this particular reporter operated. She smelled scandal where the innocent walked and heard rumour in the wind. Her word was about as reliable as a weather forecast, and Sara knew how inaccurate those could be!

It was quite obvious, she decided as she put the paper down with an outward calm, that the article had blown a publicity stunt quite out of proportion. She had worked long enough for B.J. to know how these things were arranged. A publicist got together with the media and a carefully created 'happening' seemed to occur spontaneously. She was sure if she phoned B.J. that he would tell her that the evening had been concocted for the sole purpose of promoting *Adjustments*. Her hand reached out for the telephone receiver, then halted in mid-air. B.J. hated to be bothered on a Sunday. He'd grumble and growl and he'd make her life miserable on Monday.

Sara had a moment of indecision and then came up with a satisfactory course of action. She was sure there was a reasonable explanation and she didn't think Lee would mind giving it to her. She'd go to the theatre that afternoon; the opening night was only a week away and the schedule of rehearsals had been stepped up to a frenetic pace. That way she could discuss it with him face-to-face, they'd laugh about it and Lee would once again remind her how celebrities had to live in goldfish bowls. She wasn't in the least bit anxious about his relationship with Felicia. Acting was an intimate sort of business, but it didn't necessarily lead to anything beyond the stage. Felicia and Lee were probably nothing more than good friends.

With that soothing thought, Sara dressed in a pair of jeans and black turtleneck, pulled her hair back into a chignon and joined Elissa for a late Sunday breakfast. If her cousin noticed any change in Sara's attitude, she refrained from mentioning it. Sara had a leisurely meal, read the rest of the paper, worked on the crossword puzzle and finally left for the theatre. She was in a fine frame of mind as she walked down the aisle in the darkened stalls and sat down next to the director, John Hart.

He glanced up at her and smiled. 'We don't see you here too often.'

'How many playwrights can stand watching their work produced?'

'Not too many,' he grinned. 'But you've come for a good scene. It's Lee's big number with Felicia.'

The set was the psychiatrist's office, and Sara watched as the prop people scurried back and forth on the lit stage, setting the couch at the proper angle, putting a phone on the desk, hanging a picture on the wall. The office had the affluent look of a physician

who had been highly successful and wanted it to show.
The rug on the floor was Oriental; the chair behind the
desk was large, black and seemingly made of leather;
and there was a bank of stereo equipment on a shelf. As
she watched the room take shape, Sara realised that she
had no real memory of the psychiatrist's office of her
childhood; she could only recall what had taken place
in it—as if her memory had been selective, burning
away the extraneous details and focusing on the crucial
elements.

Felicia came out on stage, and Sara stiffened. The
scene took place near the end of the play and the
scruffy, scowling adolescent of the first act had
disappeared for a young woman who was trying her
best to appear mature and more feminine. Instead of
jeans and a T-shirt, Felicia was dressed in a blue
shirtwaist and was wearing low heels. Her blonde hair
was combed neatly into a gleaming cap and her whole
demeanour suggested the desire to please. She sat down
on the couch, took a compact out of her bag and dusted
her nose. She glanced at her watch and, noticing that
she was early, stood up and moved around the set, idly
rearranging the props; the vase of flowers, the files on
the desk, the pictures on a shelf. It was all done in utter
silence, but actions spoke louder than words. Maria was
quite comfortable in the psychiatrist's office, and any
audience would understand the meaning of those small
domestic gestures. A woman liked to handle a man's
things—when she was attracted to him.

Sara's mouth had gone as dry as the desert; her
fingers gripped her knees with a desperate intensity. She
wanted to scream that it wasn't so, that she had never
acted the way Felicia was, but she was incapable of
speaking. She sat immobile in her chair as if she had
been frozen there. She didn't hear John's low murmur
of approval; her eyes were fixed on the stage as Lee
entered, his tall length dressed in casual tweeds, a pipe

in one hand. She watched him as he walked to the chair and picked up a file, opening it and then smiling at Felicia.

Sara had suffered from bad dreams and nightmares that never seemed to end, but nothing equalled the scene played out before her. It was far, far worse than watching the opening scene of the first act. That, at least, had authenticity; she had felt as if she were reviewing her life, but this was different. As Lee talked and Felicia listened, Sara saw a perverse and horrible distortion of the truth. There was an obvious element of sexuality between the psychiatrist and the young girl. He was using his masculinity to cure her, to make her respond, and Maria, still not talking, demonstrated in every line of her eager face and pliant body that she was receptive to Dr Holme's good looks and virile charm.

Lee was good. Whenever she could drag herself from the horror of what was happening on the stage back into reality, Sara realised that he was very, very good. There was nothing of the macho sex symbol in him at all. He leaned back in his chair or walked around the room, looking very much like a man who is aware of his ability as a physician. When he used his sensuality on the vulnerable Maria, it was done with calculated skill. He never touched her, but every gesture indicated his interest in her as a woman. With a sickening feeling, Sara recognised the very techniques he had used on her; that casual, devastating smile, eyes narrowed and glinting. She couldn't blame Maria for succumbing to them; she'd fallen for them herself.

The scene ended just as Sara thought she could bear it no longer and John was standing, his hands applauding. 'Great,' he was saying. 'That's great!'

Felicia, who had emerged from her pose as the adolescent Maria, was suddenly very much the professional actress, frowning with concern. 'I was wondering about that moment when Lee turns to look at me, after he says the line about my mother. I could be more obvious about how I feel about him.' And her mobile face quickly assumed an expression of longing, of awe.

Lee shook his head. 'I get the vibes, believe me.'

John agreed. 'It requires subtlety.'

Felicia smiled, her pixie face exuding sheer joy. 'You mean we've done it?' she asked.

John nodded. 'It's perfect,' he said with satisfaction. 'Absolutely perfect.'

Felicia impulsively wrapped her arms around Lee and kissed him on the mouth. 'Congratulations, Dr Holme,' she said, her voice exuberant. 'We've done it!'

Sara watched Lee pick her up and swing her around the stage, his face smiling into Felicia's, his eyes only for her. When he put her down, he began to hum and they swept into a waltz, Felicia dipping and swaying in his arms. The waltz developed into a fast tango and Felicia grabbed a flower from the vase and stuck it between her teeth as Lee bent her back over his arm. From there they moved into a hip-shaking, thighs-touching disco number that had the stage technicians laughing and slapping their knees. Throughout it all, Sara sat in numb silence. She knew Lee and Felicia were reacting to the stress of the scene, but they fitted so well together, responding to one another's moves as if they could read each other's minds, and she recognised a tie and a camaraderie between them that far exceeded anything she had felt with Lee.

They stopped, both faint with laughter, then Lee peered into the darkened audience, his eyes shaded by his hands. 'Is that Sara out there?' he asked.

John turned and saw that Sara had left. 'She was here, Lee,' he said. 'Sitting with me through the whole scene.'

'Sara!' Lee jumped down from the stage and started up the aisles. 'Sara!'

She heard him, but it was too late. She was out the side door of the theatre and walking rapidly around the corner so he couldn't find her, her breath coming fast and hard, tears streaming down her cheeks. The sun was shining on to the city pavements, the air held a hint of spring and the pigeons were strutting on the streets, pecking for food and cooing, but Sara was oblivious to anything but her own pain. It filled her, making her heart ache and her head throb, and she didn't know what she could do to ease it.

How she wished she hadn't gone to the theatre and watched Lee and Felicia play that scene. Ignorance was bliss, and she would have been far better off if she hadn't known the direction *Adjustments* was taking. She had accepted the affair between the psychiatrist and the mother now that she knew it had some basis in fact, but a sexual relationship between Maria and Dr Holme was unthinkable. It was a monstrous lie, a sexual perversion of her life.

Sara jammed her fists into the pockets of her jacket and gnashed her teeth when she realised how helpless she was. She couldn't change John's direction or Lee's interpretation. The play was due to open soon and there was nothing she could do to stop it. Anger and frustration made her breath catch in her throat and, if she had had Lee before her, Sara knew she would have eagerly wrung his neck in her bare hands.

And then there was his obvious attachment to Felicia. Sara didn't know if they were lovers, but if they weren't yet, she was sure they would be soon, and the thought of *that* seemed to tear through her insides like a huge claw. She had never known that jealousy could be so painful. She wanted to double over and clutch at her chest as if she could protect her heart, but the feeling came from within, gnawing at her like some inexorable beast. So she walked, blindly and desperately, not knowing exactly where she was, but not caring if she were lost or going in circles.

Late Sunday afternoon in the city had a slower pace; children played on the sidewalks, lovers walked hand in hand through Central Park and down Riverside Drive. The good weather had brought out the frisbee players and the joggers in full force, and Sara frequently had to stop or shift her course to make way for others. She walked for miles with her head down, her eyes on the ground and her shoulders slumped in defeat, a silent and unhappy figure weaving through the happy crowds. By the time she made it back to her apartment, weary from walking, her eyes dry and tired from crying, night had settled on to the city, the greyness of dusk softening its hard edges.

The phone was ringing when she entered the apartment, and there was a note from Elissa pinned to the telephone, saying that Lee had rung several times. Sara ignored the phone, tore up the note and went to her bedroom where she lay down and stared at the ceiling. She had learned one thing during the miles she had trudged that afternoon: that jealousy could not exist alone and that it was part and parcel of an emotion far larger and more encompassing. Love, she now understood, had many faces; sensuality, tenderness, vulnerability and jealousy. She had seen them all and ignored them to her peril. Love had crept up on her unawares and now held her tightly in its bittersweet embrace.

CHAPTER EIGHT

THERE had been various times in Sara's life when she'd felt as if she had plumbed the depths of despair, but nothing equalled the plummeting of her emotions during the week before *Adjustments* opened. The worst of it was that she had nowhere to turn for respite. B.J. was busier than he'd ever been, his three phones ringing almost continuously, his desk piled high with paper. Even Sara, who had begged off helping with the play originally, was now dragged back into work. The advance ticket sales were enormous; the public was obviously being lured by the name of Lee Cameron on the marquee. The press was in feverish speculation over the play's chances of survival, and not a day passed that Sara didn't catch sight of a mention of *Adjustments* or its stars. She had also been besieged by requests for interviews, but only granted one, and that was to the drama critic of the *New York Times*. She had met him before, and she knew that he would put a generous slant in his article. Still, it had been a shock to open the paper and see her own picture there and her name in large-print black typeface.

She barely saw Elissa during this period. She seemed to be sleeping in late after Sara left for work and coming back to the apartment when Sara was already in bed. When asked what she was up to, Elissa was evasive, and Sara began to wonder if she were involved with a man. She had never seen her cousin blush before or mumble so frequently. She had finally given up questioning her cousin, knowing that there was no point in prying—Elissa could be as stubborn as a mule—and that she would find out in good time; she had never known Elissa to keep a secret for more than a week. At any rate, she bestowed a silent blessing on her cousin, praying that the romance, if that was what it was, was travelling a smoother path than her own.

Lee still phoned her every night, but their conversations were short and terse. He was, she knew, overwhelmed with work and utterly exhausted. In addition to the constant rehearsals and interviews, Lee spent three hours exercising a day. Acting required endurance, and he jogged every morning and worked out with weights during the afternoon. When he phoned her, she could hear the fatigue in his voice, and it provided her with a good excuse to keep their conversations brief. He had asked her about coming to the theatre on Sunday, but she had brushed off her presence as mere curiosity, and when he had asked her what she thought of the scene, she had only said that it was impressive. He made no mention of Felicia, and neither did Sara. She couldn't bear to talk about it.

Love, it seemed, was the most excruciating emotion of all. She was tormented by thoughts of Lee and Felicia; of him walking with her, talking to her and, worst of all, making love to her. There seemed no end to the potential of her vivid imagination, and Sara tried everything in her power to dull her mind. She threw herself into work, thankful that the office was so hectic that no one noticed her feverish devotion to typing and filing. She spring-cleaned her apartment; she brought out all her summer and spring clothes; she reorganised her filing cabinets and her closets. She read at least a dozen mystery novels in the hope that murder would be soothing and keep her mind off love.

But ultimately, nothing could keep away the early morning depressions, the times when she awoke before the sun had risen and her thoughts turned to Lee and the way she was ruining her life. Everyone had suspected that she was in love except Sara herself. She had denied it vehemently, to the world and to herself, but now that she recognised it, she was miserable. Of all the men to fall in love with she had had to choose the most unsuitable! Lee made love to thousands of women when he was on the screen and they all loved him back in a mass adoration. And who was she but one of the adoring throng? In one sense, she was no better than sixteen-year-old Marcie Kerne; they both were in love with a man on a pedestal—a movie idol who paid them the occasional compliment of his interest. Sara was under no illusions about Lee's phone calls. He was with Felicia almost day and night; she was an afterthought.

The week crawled by, tempers rising daily as the countdown towards opening night came closer and closer. B.J. had assumed a perpetual snarl, the typing pool had hysterics at least once a day and Sara felt as if her insides were being twisted and stretched like an enormous rubber band. One afternoon, unable to bear the tension in the office for one more second, Sara announced that she had a splitting headache, went home early and found Elissa in the living room lying on the couch and reading a magazine.

'I think the office is going to explode,' Sara said with a sigh as she flopped down in a chair and then added enviously, 'You look comfortable.'

'Mid-term exams are over,' Elissa explained with a yawn, 'and I'm tired.'

Sara gave her a knowing look. 'You've been out late almost every night.'

'I've been studying,' Elissa said airily.

Sara smiled to herself, then rummaged through her bag. 'I have some tickets for opening night,' she said, 'and I've decided to invite your mother and mine.'

Elissa's blue eyes widened. 'You're asking Marion to come?'

'And Gregory,' said Sara. 'I thought I should.'

'You think she's going to like the play?'

Sara shrugged helplessly. The decision had not been as easy as she made it seem; she had thought long and hard about asking her mother to see *Adjustments*. She had no idea how Marion would react to this public rendering of her life, and at first she had decided against it, but second thoughts had finally prevailed. Sara knew that Marion would be highly offended if she wasn't invited, and perhaps Betty was right about their mutual need for discussion. Perhaps the play would be the key that would open the door on the past and on subjects that had long been verboten.

'I have a feeling it's going to be a very interesting night,' Elissa said with a tone of speculation.

'And possibly disastrous,' Sara said wryly, handing her an envelope with tickets enclosed. 'There's two for you. I thought you might want to bring someone.'

Elissa closely examined her nails. 'I might bring a date.'

Sara was equally casual. 'That's fine with me.'

'What . . . about Peter?'

'I sent him a ticket. I wasn't sure if he'd want to come or not, but it seemed like the courteous thing to do.'

'You're really finished with him, aren't you?'

Sara leaned back and closed her eyes. 'It's definitely over.'

'So you wouldn't mind if he were dating someone else?'

Sara's eyes sprang open and she stared at Elissa. 'You've seen him with someone?'

Her cousin picked up her magazine and leafed through a few pages. 'I heard that he's been going out with another woman.'

'I wonder who.' Sara sat up suddenly. 'His ex-wife!?' she asked in disbelief.

'No, a . . . a younger woman.'

'Maybe he met her at the bank,' Sara suggested.

Elissa shrugged nonchalantly. 'Could be.'

'Well, that was fast. I always thought that Peter was in love with the idea of being in love with me rather than anything more serious. I guess this confirms it.'

'Do you really think so?'

Sara yawned and missed Elissa's intense look. 'Uh-uh. If he's already dating again then I doubt if our breaking up was anything more than a dent to his ego. He's a nice man; he's going to make some lucky woman a wonderful husband.'

The office went from bad to worse, and Sara's own personal fears had her in a state of dreadful anticipation. She felt as if she had only a very tenuous grasp on her sanity, and she found herself nervously pacing her bedroom at night, wishing desperately that the play's opening were behind her instead of looming ahead in the future like some possible end to the world. She grasped at any and every opportunity to get out of her apartment, and it was this need for flight that led her to accept Lee's unexpected invitation to dinner at his place on the evening before opening night. She said yes before she thought twice, and Lee had finished the call before she had a chance to say that she had changed her mind. Sara could have phoned him back, and the rational part of her mind that usually held her in tight control was insistent that she should, but its note of caution went unheeded. Sara wanted to be with Lee; she could no more help herself than the slender reed can resist the power of a torrential river. Love had taken precedence, its inexorable and overwhelming force sweeping every hesitant thought aside like puny twigs tossed and discarded by a flood.

She dressed for dinner that night with extreme care. She wore black velvet evening pants and an ivory blouse with flowing sleeves and a lacy yoke. Her make-up was impeccable, and she knotted her hair into a smooth chignon on her neck, its gleaming coppery strands pulled back tightly from her face, a look which made her eyes seem wider, their ends tilting into the darkened fringe of her long lashes. When she arrived at the door of Lee's apartment, she looked absolutely immaculate, not a hair out of place, not a smudge on her make-up, every nail long, curved and fuchsia pink. Although she wasn't exactly aware of it, she was, in a metaphorical sense, dressed in armour. The way she appeared was merely the outward indication of a carefully thought out plan of action. She wasn't sure what Lee's invitation meant, but she was exceedingly wary of his intentions. When he opened the door, the expression on her face was cool, haughty and composed.

Lee's dark eyebrows raised to a quizzical arch. 'You don't look like an anxious playwright,' he commented.

Sara swept in past him. 'I'm not.'

'Sometimes looks are deceiving.'

'Not in this case,' she said coldly.

'I didn't know,' he replied, closing the door behind him, 'that you had nerves of steel.'

She handed him her jacket. 'What's the point in worrying?'

'How true,' he murmured as he hung her jacket in the closet. 'I keep asking myself the same question.'

Lee's apartment was opulent but subdued, with that effect that only good taste and an extravagant use of money can bring. The living room had two walls made of mirror and the other made of glass. When the dark burgundy curtains were open, as they were now, the room seemed to be an extension of the night itself, the pointed glitter of the stars and the pale disk of the moon reflected in the depths of the mirrors. There was a sunken seating arrangement of black leather cushions, thick and buttoned, and tables of rosewood and glass. Sara's high-heeled shoes sank into the plush of the cream carpet and she thought, as she stepped down into the living room, that Lee had rented a place that suited him well. They both had an aura of masculine elegance; the apartment in its rich contemporary design and Lee, dressed in well-tailored black slacks and a navy-blue silk shirt with epaulettes on the shoulders, its sleeves rolled up and held with buttoned loops.

Sara discovered that she wasn't quite prepared for the impact of his physical presence no matter how many hours she had thought about him. The incisive cut of his mouth, the width of his chest and the hint of male virility in the tight cut of his slacks made her feel faint, and she almost lost her haughty façade when Lee brushed by her on his way to a buffet that held a tray of old-fashioned glasses and several tall bottles. The brief touch of his arm against her shoulder sent a jolt right down to her toes and she had to steady herself, hand out against a wall. Desire had undermined every defence she had raised against him, and she was uncomfortably aware of every move that he made and every glance of his dark eyes.

'A drink?' he asked.

'No, thank you.' Sara didn't dare drink; she needed to keep her wits about her.

'You don't mind if I do?'

She waved a hand negligently in the air and wandered off to look out the window. She heard the clink of a glass behind her and the pouring of liquid, then Lee was standing behind her, looking with her at the brilliant skyline of Manhattan.

'Here's to New York,' he said, lifting his glass in a mock-toast. 'May it love *Adjustments*.'

'What makes you think it won't?'

'The acting, the set, the night air, how comfortable the seats are. God knows what makes one play a hit while another dies after opening night.'

Sara stared down to the street where cars, small as

toys, appeared to chase one another around corners and through lights. 'Quality, I suppose.'

Lee gave her a slanting glance. 'You really are cool, aren't you?'

'It's out of my hands,' she said with a shrug. 'I realised that long ago.'

'Do I detect a note of bitterness?'

'I lost control of *Adjustments* months ago when . . .' she hesitated.

'When I got the part of Dr Holme,' Lee finished for her, his mouth twisted wryly.

'You were wrong for the part.'

'Am I still?' he asked, his dark eyes watchful.

'What difference does it make what I think?' Sara carefully avoided his glance and stared out towards the sky where a plane moved slowly against the backdrop of black velvet, its wing tips glittering red and green as if they had been encrusted with tiny rubies and emeralds.

Lee's hand came to her chin and forced her to look at him. 'I want to know,' he said softly.

Sara forced herself to remain calm, to stop her knees from trembling, to keep any hint of love from her eyes. 'I still think you're wrong,' she said icily.

His hand dropped and he casually took a sip of his Scotch. 'I wondered why you ran away from the theatre,' he said. 'I hadn't thought you'd be a coward.'

Anger suddenly rushed through her veins. 'Wouldn't you have run,' she demanded hotly, 'when you saw your life being turned into a horrible lie?'

'You wrote the words.'

'And you're twisting them!'

Lee's mouth was hard. 'Why can't we get beyond this?'

'Beyond what?'

'This damned obstacle of the play. Is it the affair with the psychiatrist and the mother that upsets you?'

Sara paused. 'No,' she finally admitted, her voice low. 'I . . . I found out that it was true.'

To her surprise, Lee wasn't triumphant at all. 'I'm sorry,' he said sympathetically, placing his hand on her shoulder.

She couldn't bear his touch and she backed to stand by a nearby chair, her hands gripping its back until her knuckles went white. 'I took your suggestion,' she said. 'I visited my aunt and she told me . . .' Her voice trailed away and her eyes looked blindly into space.

'Told you what, Sara?' Lee's casual pose hid his sudden tension.

'That . . . that my mother had several lovers while I was growing up, and that in all probability she and my doctor were sleeping together.' Her eyes shifted and then focused on Lee. 'I suppose that makes you happy,' she added angrily.

'Why should it?'

'Because it proves your point, doesn't it? You've been saying all along that I didn't know what the hell was going on.'

His voice was gentle. 'Don't castigate yourself. It only proves that a young girl was very innocent.'

'But not so innocent that you didn't guess.'

'You wrote what you heard. It was honest reporting.'

'It was ignorant!' she snapped. 'Stupid and ignorant.'

'Sara . . .' Lee began, but he was interrupted by the sound of a bell and he put his glass of Scotch down on a table. 'Dinner's ready. My cook, Mrs Meach, prefers chimes to announcements.'

The meal was served in an alcove off the kitchen, a cosy room of glass windows and plants, filmy white curtains and white wicker chairs with blue and gold cushions. Lee explained that the dining room was too formal for two people alone, and Sara agreed. She would have felt ridiculous sitting at one end of the long rosewood table while Lee sat at the other. It was a room for elegant dinner parties and formal entertaining with its brown velvet chairs and a massive chandelier. She much preferred the small, round table with its blue cloth and gold napkins folded into miniature tents on the white plates.

The cook, short, plump and greying, laid the meal out for them, placed a tray of pastries on a buffet beside the table and plugged in the coffeepot. She accepted Lee's thanks with a smile, said that she hoped they would enjoy the meal and that she would be back the following morning. When she was gone, Lee carved Sara a tender slice of roast beef and placed it on her plate, saying, 'Mrs Meach is a gem.'

'I read that you stole her away from . . . was it the mayor?'

Lee gave her a laughing glance. 'Do you believe everything you read?'

'Are you a thief or not?' she demanded.

'I confess,' he admitted. 'She couldn't pass up the chance to work for America's sexiest man. Admit it, the mayor is dull in comparison.'

'The paper said that you offered her an outrageous salary.'

'Are you saying,' he asked teasingly, 'that my charm isn't sufficient?'

'I'm saying,' Sara retorted, 'that you're the kind of man who doesn't quit until he gets what he wants,' and then flushed when she caught Lee's dark glance with its unmistakable message.

'You think I can get everything I want?' he asked silkily.

'More rice, please.'

'You didn't answer my question.'

She gave him a level look. 'No,' she said, 'I don't think you can.'

'And what do you think I want that I can't have?'

She saw an opportunity to alter the drift of the

conversation from sexual innuendo into a subject less controversial. 'The kind of life ordinary people have,' she said. 'Most men want a wife and family; they want to deal with their feelings in a private rather than public forum.'

'I could retire,' he said.

'But you haven't,' she pointed out, accepting her plate from his outstretched hand.

'No,' he said slowly, 'but then I haven't met any woman yet who would be worth the sacrifice.'

Not even Felicia? Sara wanted to ask, but instead her tone was light and teasing. 'And think of your choice,' she said. 'Women are panting after you.'

'Adoration is boring.'

'What about those glamorous movie stars who've played opposite you?'

'Marriages between film stars rarely survive. Too much competition.'

Sara watched him reach for a bottle of wine. 'Fiona says she's never seen you serious about a woman.'

Lee gave her a mocking glance. 'Fiona is a chatterbox.'

Curiosity drove her onward, even when she knew that the answer would hurt. 'Was she right?' she asked lightly, as Lee poured the ruby-red wine into her goblet. 'She seems to know you very well.'

The look he gave her was long and enigmatic. 'Yes,' he said at last, then lifted his wine glass to the hard line of his mouth. 'To *Adjustments*,' he added, and Sara, lifting her glass, echoed his words. 'To *Adjustments*.'

As if they had agreed on some sort of a truce, Lee and Sara discussed nothing personal for the rest of the meal. It seemed safer to talk about politics and art than their feelings; at least, Sara felt that way. When Lee talked about women and marriage, she lost all sense of reality as she knew it. As far as she was concerned, Lee was involved with Felicia. She could understand why he hadn't invited her to dinner; the two of them probably needed some breathing space after the intensity of rehearsals, but Lee's words indicated that there was far less involvement than she had imagined. And if Sara had nourished any hope that Lee felt something for *her*, it was dashed by his blunt meaning – no woman was worth his career; no woman was worth more than a trivial affair.

They had coffee in the living room where she questioned him about making his first movie, the one that had catapulted him into the public eye. He had played a hard-boiled detective with unerring aim and a soft spot for pretty women, and within a few weeks of its release, he had become a household name.

'What was it like?' she asked. 'Making headlines virtually overnight?'

Lee leaned back against the black leather of the banquettes, his arm stretched across the cushions so that his hand almost touched her shoulder. When he sat down next to her, she had made sure that there was a protective space between them. Lee might not be serious about her, but she was very serious about him. Anything nearer than two feet was too close for comfort.

'I had no idea what would happen,' he said. 'I was merely glad for the chance to be in a film. I liked the story and I liked the part. It seemed enough to have gotten my foot in the door. But when the film was released and the hoopla started, I confess,' and he grinned at her, 'that my first instincts were to run like hell!'

'But it must have been gratifying. Isn't every actor after recognition?'

'Fame—we all crave fame with an obsessive mania. I wanted it so badly; there were times I thought I would kill for it. Then when it was there and my pictures were in the paper and the groupies started hanging around my apartment, I discovered it had an ugly side.' He glanced at her. 'You've seen it. That episode downtown; the crowd tearing at our clothes as if some of the glamour could rub off on to them. It's happened before. I've been scratched, gouged and mauled.'

'Is that why you're trying a stage role?' she queried.

'You think it will lower my recognition quota?' he asked wryly.

Sara shook her head. 'The stage is less accessible than the movies to the public. Most people wouldn't recognise Broadway actors.'

'No, it isn't that.' Lee ran his fingers through his dark hair. 'I needed a change of pace, a new challenge. I was damn tired of being the same man in every film.'

'So you chose something completely different,' she said softly.

'I understand it,' he said sharply. 'I know what it was like to have a father leave.'

'But it wasn't your fault!' she snapped. 'You didn't feel guilty.'

He suddenly grabbed her shoulder with his outstretched hand. 'How do you know how I felt?'

Sara was stubborn. 'You didn't precipitate your parents' break-up the way I did.'

'Every child of divorced parents has a secret guilt that they are the reasons for the split. It was egocentric of me, I know, but I was convinced that he must have hated the sight of me, because he left and never came back. None of the other fathers I knew could have ignored their children for twenty years.'

She could feel his vehemence in the strength of the lean fingers that gripped the curve of her shoulder. 'He turned up again?' she asked breathlessly.

His fingers loosened. 'Of course,' he said, his mouth twisted in bitter irony. 'As soon as I was rich and famous, he drifted back into my life for a handout. He had no money; he couldn't hold down a decent job for any length of time. He was an alcoholic, Sara—a drunk.'

'What did you do to him?' she whispered in horror, unable to repress violent images of the sort of revenge a man like Lee would take out on an enemy.

He raised an eyebrow. 'Do? What could I do? I gave him some money, took him to A.A. and hoped he would dry out. It hasn't happened as far as I know. He comes back periodically. He's pathetic really.'

There was a flat tone to his voice that made Sara say, 'You don't hate him any more, do you?'

'No. I pity him.' He turned dark, brooding eyes on her. 'But if I ever have a child of my own . . .' His voice trailed away, but Sara felt the force of his intensity and finally understood what had kept Lee aloof from any serious involvement with a woman. He had come from a broken home, and it was an experience he had no intention of repeating. For him, marriage would be a lifetime commitment and the woman he chose as his wife, as the mother of his children, would have to share his inner vision of what a family should be.

Sara turned away quickly so that he couldn't see the hurt in her eyes. She knew she wasn't the woman he would choose as a wife; she was far too mundane. And she wasn't sure that Felicia would be his choice either, but she knew he would eventually find a woman who would spark the hidden fire of his love and devotion and satisfy the longing that lay beneath the outward surface of his casual charm. She could sense an emptiness in him, a yearning for a home and family, for the kind of warmth his childhood had lacked. She understood that pain too well; it was something she held permanently within her like an unhealed wound.

'I'd better go,' she said, her eye blurring with tears so that she could barely see the delicate hands of her gold wristwatch.

'Sara.' The hand that lay by her shoulder now pinioned her wrist. 'Don't leave.'

'I'm sorry,' she said, still looking away from him and now desperate to go before she really broke down. 'Tomorrow is going to be impossible.'

Lee had moved closer to her and she felt his lips move softly against the sensitive skin of her neck. 'Please don't go.'

She could barely think straight as his mouth moved to her ear. 'I . . . have to,' she muttered.

'I need you,' he murmured. 'I don't want to be alone.'

Shocked, Sara pulled away from him and turned to meet his eyes. 'You want me to stay the night?' she asked incredulously.

A muscle leapt in his jaw; deep lines were etched from his mouth to his nose. 'I can't think about the opening. It drives me crazy.'

'You're . . . you're afraid!'

He let go of her and clenched his hands into fists. 'Wouldn't you be?' he asked harshly and, standing up, walked to the window, where he stared blindly out into the night.

Sara gazed at his rigid back, her eyes widened with astonishment. Lee had always seemed so poised and so confident that she had never guessed that he would be suffering from stage fright. She should have known, she supposed; all actors had it in one form or another, even the biggest stars. She had known a famous actress who vomited five minutes before every performance with a clockwork regularity and an internationally known mime who wrapped himself in blankets because his nerves caused him to suffer intensely from chills. Why should Lee be any different? Hadn't Fiona suggested that he was vulnerable and shy beneath his hard exterior? Sara hadn't believed her then, but the hunched twist of his shoulders and the harsh profile framed against the window now proved that she had been right.

'Lee,' she began, her voice sympathetic, 'everyone suffers from stage fright. It's nothing to be ashamed . . .'

His voice was low and harsh. 'I could be the laughing stock of the nation in two days. I can just see the headlines, can't you?'

'How would you have felt if you hadn't taken up the challenge?' she asked softly.

'Furious at myself for being such a coward.' The wide shoulders slumped slightly as if their owner was weighed down by a heavy burden. 'The same way I hate myself for being,' the words were now being painfully wrenched out of him, 'so damned afraid.'

His pain transmitted itself to Sara so strongly that she flinched at the raw exposure of nerve. She too feared the reaction of the press to *Adjustments*; it quite possibly meant the end of her writing career, but for Lee the castigation of the critics would be a degrading public humiliation. She had admired him for his courage, for taking that daunting step from the movies to the stage, and now her heart went out to him. He was a proud man and she knew what his confession must cost him. He had stripped away the macho mask for her and revealed the depths of his vulnerability. She had the sudden and overwhelming desire to hold him, the way a mother comforts a child in the warm curve of her arms.

Slowly she stood up and walked over to him. If Lee knew she was there, he made no motion of recognition, his back still tense and stiff, his eyes on the mottled ivory disc of the moon. Sara hesitantly reached out and touched him along his spine where it curved upwards to the powerful muscles of his shoulders. Lee said nothing, but she felt him tremble beneath her fingers and, encouraged by that response, she moved closer, wrapping her arms around his waist and laying her cheek against his back. For minutes they stood that way in the silent, dimly-lit room, and then Sara let her hands drift upwards so that her palms lay flat on his chest, the erratic drumming of his heart pulsating through her fingertips.

Suddenly Lee turned and his arms were about her. 'Oh, Sara,' he sighed, and his mouth descended to hers, lips meeting in tenderness. At first their kiss was simply that of a warm giving, of a man in need and a woman offering comfort. Sara ran her hand over the side of his face as if she could ease the deep grooves that had been cut by tension and fatigue, and he clung to her as if she were his only salvation, the only light in the dark night of his fear.

But as his mouth moved over hers, the kiss changed and altered, its intensity deepening as desire crept upon them, gaining in strength and purpose. His hands ran over her back and down her spine to clasp the curve of her buttocks and bring her hips closer to him. Sara melted in his arms, her body moulding to fit his, her arms tight around his neck as if she were afraid he would let her go. She forgot everything but the feel of his lips and their hard demand, the possessive caress of his hands and the warm spring of passion that welled at his touch.

Every sensation she had felt in the past weeks dimmed against the flood of desire that now ran through her veins, her bones and her muscles. When his hand rose to caress her breast, it seemed to swell beneath his touch, the sensitive tip of her nipple aching to be freed from the confinement of her bra. Heat grew in her groin at the strength of his arousal and she couldn't stop her hands from moving to his shoulders, his arms and then down to his muscular waist. She pulled the shirt out of his slacks and her fingers tangled in the soft hair at his abdomen, pausing only a second at the sharp intake of his breath, and then moving downward.

'I want you,' Lee muttered, his mouth against her throat, the words rough and insistent. He picked her up as easily as if she was a child, his arms under her knees, and carried her to the bedroom, kicking its door open with his foot. Sara only caught a glimpse of the brown and gold spread and the dark tones of furniture before the room was plunged into darkness and Lee laid her on the bed, stripping his clothes off and sinking down beside her, his hands at the buttons of her blouse. 'Damn!' he swore under his breath as his hands fumbled with the tiny, fabric-covered buttons, and Sara gave a soft laugh. Nothing mattered any more, she realised with a heady sense of exultation. Nothing mattered beyond this room, this bed and this man. The only reality that counted was his hands at her breasts and the sudden coolness as the heat of her skin was exposed to the air, causing her nipple to rise even further into the erotic heat of his mouth.

He undressed her at leisure, his hands teasing and light at first as they pulled off her slacks and the wispy fabric beneath, their feather touch almost driving her mad. He could not seem to get his fill of her, and he ran his mouth between the valley of her breasts to the silky skin of her abdomen, causing her to moan and twist against him, her legs entwining with his. When his hand finally reached and stroked the soft curve of her inner thigh, Sara held her breath at the swift and sudden rush of desire that made her tremble and pressed her against the bed with its languorous force. Her legs parted automatically; her body so ready for him, so aching and eager, that she felt no pain at the first thrust of his entrance, only an intense pleasure that spun outwards, taking her with it, into a shimmering expanse of sensuality and then hurtling her higher until she broke over its pulsating edge and fell gently, softly, into its deep, black warmth.

CHAPTER NINE

SARA woke to the sound of water running and light pouring through opened curtains. She stretched, yawned and then rolled over on to her side, her eyes still shut against the sun, the coppery-red strands of her hair picking up the rays in its depths so that there seemed to be a fire burning around the pale oval of her face. The water stopped and there was the sound of footsteps by the bed. She opened one eye and saw a tanned muscular thigh covered with dark hair in her line of vision. Then a hand reached down and tousled her hair.

'Wake up, sleepyhead,' Lee's deep voice said. 'The day of judgment has arrived.'

Sara opened both eyes, glanced around her at the eminently masculine bedroom and then sat straight up, a sheet clutched over her bare breasts. 'My God,' she whispered, 'it's morning!'

'The usual sequence after midnight,' said Lee with a smile.

Sara wasn't listening. Memories were coming back to her; Lee's arms around her, his mouth at her breast, their bodies entwined in the darkness. Her mind whirled with the kaleidoscopic rush of images; the realisation of what she had done hitting her, widening her blue eyes in horror. 'I spent the whole night here,' she whispered.

'Twelve hours,' Lee agreed lazily.

Another thought struck her. 'Elissa's going to be frantic,' she breathed.

Lee sat down on the edge of the bed and looked at her. 'Is that your cousin?'

Sara nodded.

'The young lady phoned about half an hour ago, and Mrs Meach told her you were here.'

Sara sunk down into the sheets. 'Oh, God,' she said flatly.

Lee leaned forward and pushed a tendril of hair behind her ear. 'Take it easy,' he said gently. 'You're not the first woman to spend the night at a man's apartment.'

She looked anywhere except at him. He had just taken a shower and was wearing only a brief towel around his hips, revealing the perfection of strong muscles and a deep chest with a triangle of dark hair. He looked cool and calm; his black hair was tousled, his eyes were clear and unshadowed, his mouth held its usual hard and incisive curve. She should congratulate herself, she thought with a sudden surge of irony and self-hatred, on accomplishing what she intended. From his smile, she knew that he had regained his confidence and was no longer afraid. She, on the other hand, had lost her pride and self-respect. Sex might have cured Lee, but it had left her with a feeling of loss and personal devastation that seemed almost impossible to bear.

'I never intended . . .'

'I know,' he said, 'but I'm glad you did.'

A flame of hope leaped in Sara's chest. 'Are you?' she asked.

He took her slender white hands in his lean, dark ones. 'Sara, I needed you desperately last night. I knew I couldn't be alone and face the midnight demons that would come once I thought about the play. Thank you for staying.'

Was that all? she suddenly wanted to ask, a sharp, bitter pain shooting through her and tightening around her heart like a vice, and she looked away so that Lee couldn't see its reflection in her eyes. She had followed her emotions last night; she had thrown caution to the winds and let love and compassion lead her into Lee's arms, but underneath she had had another motive. Peter had called her a fool, and he had been so right. Despite all that she knew about Lee, the casual affairs and his admittedly aloof attitude towards women, she had nursed a tiny seed of wishful thinking that he loved her in return and that their lovemaking would melt away whatever protective shield lay around his heart.

She remembered that exultation she had felt when his desire had matched hers and now found that its heady taste had gone quite sour. He had wanted her, yes, but any warm body could have done what she had. Some men drank when they were frightened, others had sex. Lee had just needed a woman to keep him company and hold his fears in abeyance. Sara had filled the slot perfectly; she'd been easy, available and willing, no different from any of the other groupies who would have leaped into his bed at the drop of a hat, thankful for the chance to spend the night with a star as famous as Lee Cameron.

She snatched her hands out of his grasp. 'I hope you're feeling better,' she said coldly, 'but I'd like to leave now.'

'Sara. . . .' He leaned forward as if he would kiss, and she shrank back against the headboard.

'Don't *touch* me,' she said quickly.

His dark eyebrows pulled together in a frown. 'You didn't mind my touching you last night.'

'Last night was different,' she retorted.

'Different? How?'

'It was . . .' Sara sought desperately for a word, anything that could conceal the pain inside and strike out at Lee. She had a sudden belief in the old biblical adage: an eye for an eye, a tooth for a tooth, having never before realised just how satisfying primitive revenge can be. 'It was curiosity,' she finally concluded.

'What the hell are you talking about?'

She laughed lightly and gave him an arch smile. 'Isn't it every woman's dream to sleep with Lee Cameron?'

For a second, she was afraid he would hit her. His teeth clenched together with an audible sound, his hands were balled into fists, and there was a glint in his eye of pure fury. Then he gained control of himself and his face took on an enigmatic look. 'Were you satisfied?' he asked in an equally blasé tone.

'Very. It was quite a performance.' Sara had never aspired to be an actress, but she thought today she would have done the Broadway stage proud. Her heart felt as if it was cracking, but she fluttered her eyelashes at him and gave him a knowing look as if they had just shared some small, dirty joke.

Lee stood up and looked away from her. 'Mrs Meach is preparing breakfast,' he said in an icy, polite tone.

'I'm ... not hungry,' Sara said. 'I'll just get dressed and leave.'

He shrugged his muscular shoulders as he walked to the closet. 'If that's the way you want it,' he said, his voice bored.

She stared at the long, straight line of his back and the muscles that rippled under the skin as he reached for a shirt. She had caressed him there, had run her hands along those very muscles and loved their feel under her fingers. A lump rose in her throat and tears misted her eyes, but she knew what she had to do and, with every ounce of will power that she possessed, she held on to the last remnant of her poise.

'That's the way I want it,' she said casually, not realising that her hands were clenching the border of the sheet at her breasts and twisting it into a tight and convoluted knot.

The lobby of the theatre was jammed with a glittering crowd of New Yorkers when Sara arrived that night and she slipped into their midst, hoping that no one would recognise who she was or want to talk to her. The day had already proven to be such a nightmare that Sara was half convinced that all her fears and trepidations about *Adjustments* were going to come true. She had left Lee's apartment for her own that morning, wondering how she was going to face Elissa and explain what happened, only to arrive and find that her cousin was gone and had left a note that she wouldn't be coming back at all that day but would see Sara at the theatre. Although admittedly relieved at Elissa's absence, Sara was afraid that her cousin hadn't been able to face her, and the thought that her cousin was ashamed added another layer of hurt to the pain inside.

She had arrived at the office late to find it in an utter turmoil, with TV cameras set up, press people swarming all around and B.J. in a decidedly foul frame of mind at the chaos. Sara was called upon to be part of an interview, answer the madly ringing telephones, solve a minor box-office crisis and sooth B.J.'s temper. They worked late and she barely had time to get back to her apartment and change for the performance. At the risk of being probably the first playwright in history to be late for her own opening, she luxuriated in a hot bath before dressing in a long black strapless sheath with a slit up one side of the skirt and a sequined black and gold bolero jacket that covered her bare shoulders. She wore her hair down, the gleaming copper strands falling in waves to her shoulders and held back from her temples with glittering ebony combs. She dressed with Lee in mind, knowing that she would have to face him at the cast party after the show and determined that he would see nothing in her appearance that would give him a clue to the unhappy state of her mind.

With every passing minute of the day, Sara had grown more and more convinced that her intuition about Lee had been correct. He had made no mention of love; he had merely, like a gentlemen, thanked her for spending the night with him. The pleasure had been mutual; Sara couldn't deny that, but its meaning went no deeper than an encounter between two people who were attracted to one another but not particularly serious about anything beyond sex itself. It had been sensation for sensation's sake, nothing more. In some ways, Sara saw her night with Lee as a mutual and degrading use of sensuality for their own selfish reasons. He wanted release from his fear; she had sought his love with her body. It didn't help much, but she knew that she wasn't the first woman who had tried to ensnare a man with sex in the misguided belief that she was unique and different from all other women.

Every part of her hurt with the knowledge of Lee's indifference but, at the moment, Sara's pride was hit the hardest. She pictured Lee laughing at their night together; she was, she knew, inexperienced and probably awkward. It had been the first time she had ever slept with a man, and she had quite obviously failed. In comparison with Lee's other women, she rated herself near the bottom of the list and flinched when she thought how bad she must have been. Chalk it up to experience, she tried to tell herself, and prayed that it would eventually fade in her mind so that she could push it into oblivion. She could thank her lucky stars that there was little chance of pregnancy. Lee, of course, had assumed that she was experienced enough to practice birth control; he would never know that she had succumbed so passionately to his lovemaking that she had never given any thought to the future.

'Sara! We've been looking all over for you.'

She turned to find Marion behind her with Gregory holding her arm, and the knot tight within her seemed to take another painful twist when she saw her mother's face and knew that another moment she had dreaded was fast approaching. They hadn't seen one another in two years; they had perhaps spoken or written only a couple of times during that period. They had little in common except the past and its unpleasant memories, and it now occurred to Sara that she had been a fool to think that *Adjustments* could bring them back together. She couldn't see Marion reacting to the play with anything but shock and horror, and she bitterly regretted the impulse that had made her send out the invitation.

'Mother, how nice to see you,' she said coolly, leaning forward and kissing Marion on the cheek. Sara had quite forgotten how pretty her mother was. She was a slender woman of middle height with blonde hair, now dyed, that she wore pulled back from her face and shoulder-length. She had a patrician face with small, delicate features and wide blue eyes that Sara had inherited, and she always dressed with beautiful taste. Tonight she wore a long grey gown with a high collar embroidered with pearls that emphasised her still lovely figure, and she was kissing Sara back as if she were truly delighted to see her.

'And Gregory.' They shook hands. Her mother's husband was tall and distinguished with close-cropped grey hair, a rugged face and a demeanour that still smacked of military authority.

'I had no idea that you were writing until you sent us the tickets,' her mother said. 'How thrilling to have a play on Broadway!'

Sara gave them both a smile that hid her dismay. She had a feeling that Marion was going to be more angry than excited when she discovered just how closely the play paralleled her life. 'I hope the critics like it,' she said.

'They're bound to with this cast,' Gregory said admiringly. 'How'd you manage to snare a star like Lee Cameron?'

It wasn't easy to talk about the man she had just spent the night with. 'He ... wanted to try the stage,' she said, then hesitated. 'The play is sort of about us, Mother. I mentioned it in the letter, but I'm not sure ...'

Marion waved her hand in the air. 'Betty told me it was about the divorce. I'm past that now, Sara. It won't bother me.'

Gregory patted Marion's arm with affection. 'Your mother and I have no secrets, do we, darling?'

Sara saw her mother and Gregory exchange a warm smile, and she suddenly realised that like her father, Marion had found real and lasting happiness in her second marriage. Sara was used to her mother as a woman of nerves and tension, easily upset and highly flammable. It was one of the reasons they had never talked much in the past; fights between them had sparked too readily, but now she sensed a change. Under Gregory's influence, Marion had become calmer and more serene, the lines of strain that had been in her face when Sara was growing up were less harsh and there was a sparkle in the blue eyes that Sara had never seen before.

The lights in the lobby dimmed three times, and Sara took a deep breath. 'Here we go,' she said, giving them a nervous smile. 'Let's find our seats. We're sitting together in the front.'

'Now, don't worry,' said Gregory, tucking Marion's arm through one elbow and Sara's through another. 'We're rooting for you.'

Sara smiled up at him, thankful for kindness from a man that she barely knew and hardly recognised as a stepfather. As they walked down the aisle to the front row of the orchestra, she was glad for the support of his arm and her mother's cheerful chatter. She had a constriction in her throat and her heart seemed to beat so loudly that she wondered why no one could hear it but herself. It was her first play on Broadway; the first thing she'd written to be a success. She found that she didn't care at all about the way the play had changed from her own conception, she only cared that the audience, the huge masses of people now busily filing into their seats, their voices rising to a dull roar, would love it and understand that her life force had been poured into it, her happiness and despair revealed for their own enjoyment.

The house lights went down, the audience quieted and the curtain lifted. Constance stood on the stage and began to move as if she were oblivious to all the faces that watched her. She flicked dust off a table, altered the angle of a picture and rearranged the placing of a chair. The audience waited while she repeated herself and then, when she once again went through the same series of motions, Sara could feel the sudden quickened interest of those sitting next to her. Constance, as Donna Evans, was obviously upset; the silence dragging at her and stretching her nerves to the breaking point. When the door finally slammed, Constance wasn't the only one who flinched. Most of the audience flinched with her, and Sara knew that they were hooked.

From Maria's entrance to the moment when the curtain came down at the end of the second act, a pin could have been dropped in the audience and heard over their silence. There was a minimum of coughing and shuffling; the audience strained for every word that Lee or Constance spoke. Felicia's mute performance had them at the edge of their seats, watching her every move. Sara couldn't deny that the whole play hung together under John's direction. She almost forgot that it was her own life she was watching; the psychiatrist's manipulation and seduction of the mother fitted in quite neatly with Maria's burgeoning sexuality. You couldn't like Dr Holme; he was almost sinister in his manipulations, but he was admirable in the pursuit of his purpose. When Maria finally spoke and said, 'I love you,' flying into her mother's arms, it was quite obvious to the audience that the words had been directed to the man who had so skilfully made her aware that she was a woman.

As the curtain came down and the applause began, Sara blinked in confusion. She had the dizzying sensation that the world had shifted to the point that the play was reality and her own memories were fiction. The way Lee had played Dr Holme seemed quite logical now and everything else followed in a rational progression; Maria's response, the mother's weepy satisfaction, even the psychiatrist's triumphant professional success. Lee had made Dr Holme's motives seem quite altruistic; Maria had been cured, the end obviously justifying the means.

Sara shakily stood up to join in the standing ovation as the curtain lifted again to reveal Lee, Constance and Felicia taking their bows. What was the truth? she wondered as she stared at Lee's hard profile. Was she the Maria of the play or was she the Sara that she remembered? What had really happened to that thirteen-year-old girl, and what had she buried so deeply in her mind that the grown-up Sara couldn't find it?

It frightened Sara to think that a part of her was missing, lost in some inaccessible twist of her brain, and she turned to Marion with a sudden urgency, only to find that her mother was clapping wildly, tears forming a glittering path down her cheeks. Sara looked away, stunned and shocked. She had expected everything from cold anger to white-hot fury, but she had never anticipated that *Adjustments* would make Marion cry. Sara impulsively took her mother's hand in hers, a thin slender hand weighted down with rings, and felt it tighten in hers. They didn't look at one another; they stared at the stage, but this small, silent communication spoke louder than words, and the love that Sara held for her mother, long stifled and repressed, broke out from its restraints and filled her heart with a sudden joy.

The applause went on and on, one curtain call after another. Lee, flanked by both actresses, constantly smiled at the audience, but Sara could see the perspiration on his brow and the lines of fatigue around his mouth. She wanted to hate him, but found that she couldn't. She knew what this triumph meant to him and how intense his drive to success had been. Lee deserved this moment, and only she would ever know that it had been underlain by a crisis of confidence. Lee wasn't the type of man to confess his fears to anyone, and she suspected that she was the first woman in his life he had ever turned to for comfort, fear making him tremble in her arms. She watched him step forward and raise his hands to the audience, the gesture bringing forth an even greater frenzy of clapping, and thought that his was a secret she would keep forever. She was neither malicious nor cruel; no one would ever know how frightened Lee Cameron had been.

Suddenly she heard her name spoken over the loudspeaker and she was being pulled by a stagehand from her seat and led up on to the stage, where she joined the others. Constance hugged her and Felicia took her hand, whispering congratulations. Someone ran out from the wings and shoved a bouquet of roses into her arms. Sara, flushed and trembling, finally faced the audience and stared out into the crowd of pale faces, allowing the swell of their yelling voices and applause to break over her. For the rest of her life, she would never forget her own moment of glory and the realisation that this adulation was for her and her alone.

The curtain finally came down after a dozen curtain calls and the stage was swamped with well-wishers and fans. B.J. grabbed Sara and gave her a bear-hug, which alone made the opening a blue-ribbon occasion. In all the time she had worked for him, B.J. had never shown the slightest bit of affection.

'Baby, we've got a hit on our hands! You'll be able to retire.'

It hadn't occurred to Sara that *Adjustments* would bring in so much money that she would never have to work again, but the thought of it made her smile. 'Do I detect even the hint of regret at losing me?' she asked.

'Harumph!' he snorted. 'I'd rather have you writing plays than answering my phone.'

'What about my cheerful face in the office? Won't you miss that?'

'Stephanie's will do,' he grumbled, and Sara grinned, knowing that it was hopeless. Fishing compliments out of B.J. was like pulling hen's teeth, and everyone knew they didn't exist.

The cast party was as much of a mob scene as backstage had been. Sara lost sight of her mother and Gregory and never did find her aunt or Elissa. The crowd flowed from the theatre to a hotel one block away where B.J. had rented the ballroom for a great celebration. Sara had earlier teased him for being a cockeyed optimist, but now she realised that B.J. had just been thinking big in his usual entrepreneurial fashion. If *Adjustments* had been a flop, the party wouldn't have taken place at all and the rent for the ballroom would have been considered a business expense, but now that the play had all the characteristics of a smash, hundreds of people wanted to celebrate.

B.J. caught her at the door of the ballroom, placed a firm hand under her elbow and led her through the crowd, introducing her to directors, publishers, socialites and anyone who counted in Manhattan. Sara had gone from being B.J.'s employee to being one of his properties, and she knew that he wanted her to be seen and talked to. Now that one hit of hers was under his belt, B.J. was already working overtime on the next one.

As they made their way around the room, Sara occasionally caught sight of Lee. He held a glass of champagne in his hand and had thrown one arm around Felicia. At one point, she saw them exchanging toasts and quickly looked away, trying to concentrate on a woman who was talking to her about new trends in theatre. She smiled, she nodded, she even managed to speak one or two coherent sentences, but nothing could erase the image of their smiling faces. Anger and jealousy cut at her like a two-edged blade, causing her breath to come short until even B.J. looked down at her in concern.

'You okay?' he asked.

She shook her head. 'I think I'd like to sit down,' she said. 'I feel a bit dizzy.'

He let her go and Sara, making her way out of the ballroom, sat down on a bench at the edge of the doorway and leaned her head against the wall, closing her eyes and wishing the evening was over. She should never have come to the cast party; she should have begged off and gone home. She had known that seeing Lee again would be torture, and his obvious indifference towards her just turned the screw that much tighter. When she had gone up on the stage to take her share of the acclaim, he had looked away from her, his eyes cold in the smiling mask of his face. She felt his hostility and knew just how badly she had hurt him. He despised the women who fawned on him because they were star-struck, and Sara, lashing out at him in her pain, had hit his most vulnerable point. She couldn't blame him for hating her; she knew she had paid him the ultimate insult.

'Sara, are you all right?'

She opened her eyes to find Elissa sitting next to her,

her blue eyes full of concern, a worried expression beneath the freckles. 'I'm fine,' she said.

'You don't look it,' Elissa said bluntly.

'It's been quite a night,' Sara acknowledged.

Elissa gave her a shrewd glance. 'And the one before?'

Sara didn't know what to say. 'I'm sorry I didn't phone ... I should have, I know, but I ...'

'I'm not your mother,' said Elissa, rolling her eyes in exasperation. 'I don't care if you missed your curfew.' The ludicrous aspect of it hit them both at once and they smiled at one another. 'Sara, I just wanted to know if you were all right. I knew you were attracted to Lee, but you were so antagonistic about him that I didn't think you would ...'

Sara filled in the pause. 'Spend the night with him,' she said wryly.

'And,' Elissa looked towards the ballroom, 'now he seems to be involved with Felicia Stevens. It's none of my business, but ... Sara, I don't want you to get hurt.'

Sara patted her hand. 'You're too late, but thanks anyway.'

Elissa's face twisted in sympathy. 'He's a louse!' she said fiercely.

'I'll ... I'll never go to one of his movies again.'

Sara gave her cousin a tremulous smile. 'Your one-woman boycott will be very helpful.'

Elissa took her hand. 'Oh, Sara, I wish I could do something!'

'It's nice of you, but ...' she glanced downward. The third finger of Elissa's left hand sported a large marquise diamond with two small brilliants at either side, and Sara stared at it and then at Elissa, who had flushed redder than her hair. 'Is that an engagement ring?'

'I didn't know how to tell you, but I ... well, Peter

and I got engaged tonight.' The words came out in a rush as if Elissa had practised them over and over.

'Peter?'

'We've been going out together almost every day since you two broke up.'

Sara shook her head in astonishment. 'But I never guessed you even cared about Peter. I thought you had a sisterly sort of affection for him.'

'I did because I thought Peter was yours,' said Elissa, leaning forward earnestly, 'and when he started taking me out ... well, I figured we were buddies and that was all. At first, he spent a lot of time talking about you, but the more he did, the more we both realised how much of his feelings about you came from your resemblance to Karen. We've always liked one another, Sara. Somewhere along the line,' her blush deepened, 'we found out that we were in love. It was quite sudden and I had no intention of getting married, but ...'

A deep voice broke in. 'She threw herself immediately into my arms.'

Elissa looked up and positively dimpled. 'I did not,' she retorted, 'I waited at least fifteen minutes.'

Sara glanced up at Peter, saw the loving smile he was giving Elissa and understood just how well the two of them fitted together. She had always thought that Peter needed a woman with a sense of humour who could poke him out of his lethargy, and hadn't she recently decided that Elissa required the steadiness and perspective of a man who wasn't part of her musical world? In many ways it was a perfect match, and she only wished she had seen its potential earlier. She would have been able to avoid a lot of heartache.

'You don't mind, Sara, do you?' Elissa was asking.

'Mind? I think it's wonderful!' She hugged Elissa and, then standing up, gave Peter a very sisterly kiss on the cheek. 'Welcome to the Morrison family. We're all a bit batty—but I'm sure you've figured that one out already.'

'I did meet Elissa's mother,' Peter said with a laugh.

'And he thought I was thoroughly crazy,' Betty had joined them and she now rapped Peter lightly on the arm with her programme, 'but he likes cats, so he can't be all that bad. Now, scat you two—I want to talk to my niece.'

As Peter and Elissa walked off, laughing, with their hands entwined, Sara couldn't help sighing. She was happy for them, but the emotion was tinged with envy. Theirs was the kind of relationship she had wanted with Lee, and she knew how unlikely that was. Hell would freeze over first.

'Regrets?' asked Betty.

Sara shook her head. 'They're perfect together.'

'Mmmm, I thought so, too. He's a bit older than she is, but he's steady and she needs that.' It was Sara's turn to get rapped by the programme. 'Now about the play. Have you spoken to Marion yet?'

'No, but I will.' Sara smiled at her aunt, enjoying her bossiness and knowing that underneath that vast bosom enclosed in a gown of black silk that had seen better days beat a heart of pure, unadulterated gold.

'What about your young man?'

'Peter?' asked Sara with a frown. 'He just . . .'

'Heavens, no! Lee Cameron.'

Sara couldn't help her blush. 'He's not *mine* at all.'

'Very sensitive, I'd say. He understands women.'

'That's his stage persona,' Sara said stiffly.

'Different in real life, is he?'

She sighed helplessly. Sometimes her aunt's conversation resembled a maze with peculiar twists, odd turns and absolute dead-ends; at other times, she could be as forceful and as direct as a train hurtling down a tunnel.

'Did you like the play?' she asked, hoping for a diversion.

'It was excellent. Now, no evasions, please. I get the strong feeling that you got your wings singed a bit.'

Sara had the sudden urge to confide in her aunt. She knew of no one else who would be less censorious or more understanding about her night with Lee. For all her strange ways, Betty seemed to have a special wavelength to the human heart. Nothing shocked her, and her advice was always to the point.

Sara took a deep breath. 'I got burnt,' she admitted.

'Did you sleep with him?'

Sara nodded.

'Any chance of a pregnancy?'

Sara shook her head.

'Are you in love with him?'

'Yes,' Sara whispered.

'So it's that blonde in there, the girl who played Maria.'

Betty, as usual, had honed right in to the crux of the matter. 'I think he's in love with her,' Sara said.

'Balderdash and cat's feathers!'

'Well, he isn't in love with *me*.'

'I'm not exactly a relic from the Stone Age, you know. I've been keeping an eye on him, and I'd say he's using Felicia to make you jealous.'

Sara shook her head. 'He ... hates me. We said terrible things to one another.'

Betty gave her a severe look over her granny glasses. 'Since when do you expect love to be easy? You have to work at it, talk out your problems.'

'You don't understand,' Sara cried.

'What I understand is that a niece of mine doesn't have the gumption to go in there and fight for the man she wants. What has that blonde number got that you don't?'

'Talent . . .'

Betty snorted. 'You wrote the play.'

'She's from Lee's world; she's more suitable for him.'

'Sara, you're just being damned foolish. Why would an actor want to marry an actress? It would be a collision course of egos. Lee's interested in you and has been all along.'

'But . . .'

'Take Sheba, for instance. She wants to rule the roost. Do you think she hangs around with Solomon? Not on your life. They'd be clawing each other's eyes out. Elijah's more her style; he's easy on her nerves.'

Sara couldn't help laughing.

Betty ignored her. 'Now, get your act together and get back into that room. Walk right up to Lee and let him know you're alive and kicking.'

'I don't think . . .'

'No more banana bread and free advice.'

Sara heaved a deep sigh and, leaning forward, kissed her aunt on her soft cheek. 'All right, but you're a bossy-boots, and it's about time someone told you,' she said affectionately.

Betty sniffed. 'Someone in this family has to have some backbone.'

Sara walked back into the ballroom with her head high and a smile on her face, a slender figure in her black gown, her hair reflecting the gleam of the chandelier in its coppery-red depths. She was there to find Marion and Gregory in the crowd, nothing more and nothing less; she had no intention of following Betty's advice. Her aunt had no idea just how terrible the morning had been or with what vengeance she and Lee had cut one another. Sara saw it as an irrevocable split that nothing would repair. She had said the unforgivable, and Lee had made it quite obvious that as far as Sara was concerned, he had completely lost interest.

'Sara, congratulations! I loved the play.'

She turned to find Fiona beside her, the older woman elegant as always in a rich red gown with diamonds at her throat. 'Thanks,' she said.

'And Lee was marvellous, don't you agree?'

'Yes,' Sara agreed, 'I do.'

'If you're looking for him, he's right over there.' Fiona waved towards a corner of the ballroom through a crowd of people, and Sara inadvertently turned her head in that direction.

Lee was there, surrounded by adoring fans and signing programmes. He'd changed out of his costume as Dr Holme and was dressed completely in black, shirt open at the collar, jeans with silver studs at the hip, emphasising the narrowness of his waist and the long, muscular length of his legs. She had forgotten how she loved the lean, arrogant line of his jaw and the way his black hair lay ruffled on his forehead as if he had run his fingers through it in a fit of thoroughly masculine distraction. As she watched him, Lee leaned against a chair, casually jamming one hand in a pocket, the other gesturing as he spoke, and Sara's mouth went dry when she remembered the way those hands had touched her.

He turned then and caught sight of her, their eyes meeting across the yards of ballroom. Sara felt herself freeze in space, her hands clenched at her sides, her chin lifting to a defiant angle. Even at this distance, she could feel the intensity of his dislike, his black brows pulling together in a frown, the hard mouth twisting into a bitter slant. There was nothing left of the man she had known who could be gentle and tender; that part of Lee had been burned out by anger. All that remained was this harsh stranger with his look of contempt and disdain.

And then, just as if it had been staged, Felicia ran up to him and threw her arms around his neck. He looked down at her, still frowning, and she tilted her head questioningly at him as if to ask what was making him so cross. His smile was reluctant and, for a brief second, he glanced up to see if Sara was still watching. Then his smile widened and he pulled Felicia up to him, his dark head bending over her small, eager face. They kissed to applause, while Sara cringed as if she had been cruelly slapped in the face. She knew that Lee wanted to humiliate her, to grind her beneath the heel of his fury, and what better way to prove his involvement with Felicia than with a very public, very intimate embrace?

Sara turned on her heel and began to walk as quickly as she could in the opposite direction. She didn't notice anyone around her and barely felt the hand that tugged at her arm. She forgot that her mother would be looking for her; she no longer cared that the party was for her as well as the cast; and she had lost all desire to stay for that traditional theatre ritual – the reading of the early morning reviews. Sara wanted nothing more than to escape. She felt as if the room were suffocating her, as if she couldn't breathe . . .

'Sara, wait!'

It was Fiona who held her arm, her dark eyes beseeching. 'I don't think Lee meant what it seemed,' she said hurriedly. 'Felicia means nothing to him. They're just friends.'

Sara glanced at Fiona's agonised expression and knew that the older woman was engaged in wishful thinking. Perhaps, she didn't approve of Felicia; perhaps, she thought it would be a disastrous match. Either way, she was only hoping that there was nothing behind that obviously passionate kiss.

'I'm sorry,' she whispered and, shrugging off Fiona's hand, ran into the corridor and then fled.

CHAPTER TEN

'SARA, you really look quite ill. Are you sure you've recovered from last night?'

Sara blinked and then gave her mother a wan smile. 'Just tired,' she said. 'Too much excitement.'

Marion gazed into her daughter's face where the purplish shadows under her eyes battled for prominence with the freckles that seemed to stand out against the pallor of her skin. 'Have you suffered from dizzy spells before?' she asked in concern.

'I'm fine, really. I just found the ballroom so hot and close.'

'B.J. said you went quite pale all of a sudden.'

Sara shook her head. 'I think I was just suffering from an overdose of nerves. I don't have a Broadway opening every night of the week.'

'No, you don't. Gregory and I are so proud of you.'

Marion meant what she said; there wasn't a hint of anger or recrimination in her voice, merely pleasure and pride, and a weighty feeling of apprehension lifted from Sara's chest. She leaned back and closed her eyes against the sun. 'It's pleasant here,' she said.

Marion agreed. 'Gregory has always preferred this hotel.'

They were seated on a balcony of Marion's hotel suite that overlooked an inner courtyard that held a small fountain and several slender trees. Beams of the late morning sun slanted downward and touched on the spray of water from the fountain, turning it into a cascade of diamonds. The noise of the Manhattan street traffic could barely be heard through the surrounding buildings, and a lone sparrow swooped down from the overhead patch of blue sky to strut and peck at the freshly overturned soil in the tiny garden. Sara, who had spent one of the worst nights of her life trying to escape from the memory of Lee's cruelty, was surprised to find that for the moment she felt nothing but peace.

They were sharing a brunch; the balcony had two chaise-longues and a low table that held a tray of coffee, croissants and jellies. Gregory had a business appointment and Marion had met Sara alone, dressed in a stylish beige cashmere sweater and matching light wool slacks. As always, her mother looked impeccable and for a while Sara had her usual feeling of intimidation. All the time she had been growing up, she had been aware that Marion was far prettier than she would ever be. She had a delicate, Dresden-type beauty that men found attractive, and whenever Sara had compared herself to her mother, she had felt nothing but self-disgust. She was too tall, her hair too red, her freckles too obvious and her mouth too large. But now she saw that Marion was getting older; there were wrinkles around her eyes and a softening of skin at her throat. For the first time, Sara no longer saw her mother as physical perfection, and she wondered how much of the antagonism she had felt for Marion simply stemmed from a feeling of inferiority and an unconscious competition on every possible level.

'Did you really like the play?' she asked shyly.

'I loved it. It was so moving.'

'You didn't mind that it was about us?'

Marion smiled and pushed back her fall of blonde hair. 'It wasn't exactly me or you up there on the stage. I didn't feel as if I were seeing my life before my eyes; I just felt echoes of the past.'

Sara turned so she could watch her mother more closely. 'It didn't happen that way?'

'It did; you had the facts down pat, but the emotional context was different. I was far less upset about the divorce, for example. I'd wanted it for years. If you hadn't given me the chance to tell your father to get out, quite possibly we'd still be living together and tearing one another apart.'

Sara gaped at her. 'I gave you the chance?'

'When you told me he wanted out.'

'But . . .'

'Sara, the doctor told you that you weren't the cause of our divorce—and believe me, you weren't,' Marion said firmly. 'Your father and I were on a horrible treadmill. He thought I had my claws into him for life and would never let him go; I thought he'd never leave because of you. What you said that day was merely the catalyst for the separation.'

'I made it up, you know.'

It was Marion's turn to look surprised. 'Made what up?'

Sara shrugged. 'I lied. Maybe, that's why I felt so guilty. I wanted Dad to leave and take me with him.'

'Oh, Sara,' Marion sighed. 'You were so difficult!'

Sara was silent, her thoughts turning inward as she remembered that afternoon, that horrible afternoon when it all began. She had come home from school with some half-baked childish idea that she would make herself a blue dress with a white collar and cuffs, similar to one that a friend had worn and sewn herself. She had been full of admiration for her friend's ability and had enthusiastically decided that she could do the same herself. It hadn't seemed to matter that they didn't own a sewing machine or that she didn't know how to stitch a seam. On the school bus, she had come up with solutions to all the problems; they'd rent a machine or borrow one, she'd follow the instructions—after all, if Sandy could do it why couldn't she? She had visions of the dress already and herself in it, swirling before the mirror, her long red hair pulled back in a ribbon of matching blue.

She had really neat sandals with multi-coloured straps and . . .

'You don't know how to sew,' Marion had objected, 'but if you'd like to take lessons . . .'

Sara had been stubborn. 'Sandy did it,' she insisted.

'Sandy's mother sews all the time. I suspect that she gave her some help.'

'She did it herself.'

'I'm glad Sandy's so talented, but you'll have to start from scratch.'

'You never let me do *anything*,' Sara wailed. 'Sandy's mother lets her do whatever she wants.'

Marion began to get angry. 'You're not Sandy,' she said coldly.

'I wish I were,' Sara flung at her. 'I wish I were anything but me! I hate this family!'

'You don't have much choice.' Marion began to walk away.

'And I wish you weren't my mother either! I hate you and . . . and so does Daddy!'

'What are you talking about?' At this point Marion turned around and grabbed her by the shoulders. 'What did Daddy say?'

Sara was frightened then at the sudden look of intensity in her mother's face and immediately regretted what she had said. She knew she was lying; her father never talked about Marion to her, but she couldn't tell her mother that. Instead, she jutted out her lower lip and looked sullen.

'Tell me!' Marion shook her until her head wobbled on her neck. 'I know you and your father must talk about me. Now, tell me, dammit!'

Sara's thoughts were frantic as she tried to come up with a likely story. 'He . . . he said that he wanted to leave the house and go to live somewhere else.'

'That bastard!'

'He is not!' Sara hadn't known precisely what a

bastard was, but she knew it was bad and she began to cry. 'He hates you and so do I. I hope he does leave and . . . and I want to go with him.'

Of course, it hadn't happened that way at all. Sara hadn't witnessed the quarrel that ultimately led to her father's departure, and she'd been mortified and furious when he hadn't taken her with him, but she hadn't dared tell him that. She was sweet and loving and agreeable whenever she was with him, and absolutely terrified underneath that each visit or phone call would be his last. If he could leave her mother, why couldn't he leave her? It was a childish sort of logic, but Sara believed in it, and all the anger and frustration she had felt towards her father had to be directed somewhere. Marion had, unfortunately, been its recipient.

They fought constantly, every battle worse than the last. When she looked back at that time of her life, Sara could see how impossible she had been. She'd done her best to be stubborn, argumentative and horrible. Marion, in turn, had been going through an equally difficult time. She might have wanted Bill out of the house, but the separation was acrimonious and there had been no respite from the arguing. It had merely moved into the realm of the lawyers' offices.

Sara's unhappiness and her mother's tension had been an imflammable mixture. Sparks flew between them over the slightest issue, and the house had often been filled with the sound of raised voices and slammed doors. Their ultimate collision had occurred over a piece of burnt toast and then escalated to a confrontation over messy bedrooms, inconsiderate children, restrictive adult policies, and finally Sara's accusation that Marion had thrown her father out.

'It's your fault!' her mother had screamed at her. 'You're the one who told me he wanted to go!'

After that, Sara had not spoken for a week. She couldn't; her throat would swell painfully when she tried to talk and she was unable to utter a sound. At first, Marion had attributed it to stubbornness, but when Sara's teacher had phoned her in concern and the mother of another thirteen-year-old had asked if Sara were sick, she had taken Sara first to the family doctor and then to an ear, nose and throat specialist who had shaken his head in mystification and suggested psychiatric help.

Sara now glanced at Marion. 'I was difficult,' she agreed, 'but I couldn't help it.'

'No, it was a hard situation for everyone, and you were only a child. I wanted to help you, but I was caught in my own emotional tangle.'

Marion's candid revelations led Sara to the next question. 'You did have an affair with my psychiatrist, didn't you?'

'Yes.' They were adults now, and Marion was treating her like one. 'He was very kind and very sweet and very supportive. I needed him.'

'Did you know that Dad was sleeping with the librarian?'

'You've learned everything, haven't you?' Marion's blue eyes were sympathetic. 'I'm sure it hasn't been easy.'

'I was shocked at the way *Adjustments* turned out,' Sara admitted. 'I thought I was writing one story and the director turned it into another one.'

Marion picked up a croissant and buttered it. 'The only part that was absolutely out of whack was the way Lee portrayed Dr Holme. Your doctor wasn't like that; he was older and very laid-back. He didn't have that sensual intensity and he didn't try to cure you by making you respond to his masculinity.'

Sara suddenly leaned forward, a sensation in her chest making her feel breathless. 'He didn't?'

Marion, who was now opening one of the small bottles of jam, didn't notice the avid expression on

Sara's face. 'No, darling, he didn't. You fell in love with him; it was a puppy crush and loaded with adolescent sexual feelings. That's quite common, you know. Patients often fall in love with their doctors.'

It was as if Marion had turned a key, unlocked a door and opened it wide to let in the sweeping rush of memories. Sara began to remember things, gestures she had forgotten, an incident here and there, moments of feeling that she had suppressed beneath layers of forgetfulness. Of course, she had been attracted to her doctor; he was more fatherly than her father and the only reliable figure in a world of shifting relationships and terrifying possibilities, but the attraction had frightened her. What began as a daughterly feeling soon grew far more serious. She had dreamt of touching him, then kissing him, and finally sleeping with him.

At twenty-four, Sara was old enough to realise that there was nothing wrong with a young girl's adolescent sexual fantasies, but at thirteen she had felt a shame so pervasive that she had buried it as deep within her subconscious as it could go. For years the emotions had remained submerged beneath the cool surface of her life, until Lee had raked and stirred them up, like smouldering coals from an old fire. Blindly and instinctively, Sara had sought to conceal the disturbing memories and their emotions, fighting any suggestion that her past was different from how she had described it. Now she understood why she had fought Lee with such intensity and fury. It was self-defence; everywhere the flames touched, they had burnt her.

Marion and Gregory had to leave on an afternoon shuttle for Washington, so Sara didn't stay much longer with her mother, but there was a new feeling between them when they parted, a mutual recognition that they had passed an important crossroads in their relationship as mother and daughter. Sara knew that it would take more than a candid conversation to repair all the harm and destruction of the past, but she also knew that Marion was her enemy no longer. In fact, she had never been one; Sara was more than ready to admit that most of the hostility had been generated on her own part. Marion might have risen to anger easily, but Sara was equally at fault. She saw now that she had spent most of her adolescence forcing her mother into positions of conflict.

'Perhaps I'll visit Washington soon,' said Sara as Marion saw her to the door.

'We'd love to have you.' She paused and then added hesitantly, 'Take care of yourself, won't you?'

It was a mother's cry of caring, and Sara never knew how much she had wanted the sort of concern only a mother can offer. 'I'm . . . sorry,' she said awkwardly. 'I wish . . .'

'Hush,' said Marion, and, putting her arms around Sara, gave her a tight hug. 'Let's forget about the past and start with now.'

They both had damp eyes when they parted, but Sara left the hotel with a lighter step. If some of her problems had solutions, then perhaps the rest would be as simple to solve. She'd get over Lee; Sara knew that. She wasn't the type of person to pine for ever, and surely there were other fish in the sea. She'd made a mistake by falling in love with the wrong man and then compounded it by sleeping with him. But she didn't regret her loss of innocence as much as she regretted her loss of illusion. She had always dreamt that sex, for her, would be a part of love, of waking up next to a man who would be her life companion. She had envisaged tenderness and caring, shared showers and breakfasts in bed, long walks in Central Park and humorous arguments over who would have the first crack at the *New York Times* Sunday crossword puzzle. She had never thought that the man she first slept with would

use her as a diversion or that the morning after the
night before would include a bitter argument and a
cruel parting of the ways.

She was every bit the fool that Peter had called her
and even more so, Sara decided as she put the key into
the lock of her apartment and threw the latch. Perhaps
it was just a matter of ridding herself of girlish dreams
and facing reality. Perhaps it was time that she grew up
and discovered that men were far different from . . .

'I wondered whether you were coming home.'

Sara snapped her head around at the sound of the
deep male voice that was issuing from the living room
and, with a feeling of disbelief, she walked through its
doorway and stared at the man who appeared to be
sitting so comfortably on *her* couch, his stockinged feet
up on *her* coffee table, his masculine aura quite visibly
disturbing the serenity of *her* apartment. He wore the
same silver-studded black jeans and black shirt that he
had worn at the cast party, and Sara discovered that
she had developed quite a sensitivity to the colour
black. An allergy, in fact.

'What are you doing here?' she asked, her voice
hostile.

'Reading the paper.' Lee gestured at the newspaper at
his side.

'How did you get in?'

'Your cousin is a friend in need. She not only let me
in, but she also graciously departed so we could be
alone.'

Sara put her handbag down, tossed her coppery hair
from the shoulders of her blue turtleneck sweater and
ran her hands nervously over the thighs of her white
cords. 'Leave,' she said, pointing in the direction of the
front door. 'We don't have any reason for being alone.'

Lee crossed his arms and smiled at her lazily. 'There
are some things that two people shouldn't talk about in
public.'

'Such as?' she queried coldly.

'Sex, double beds, birth control . . .'

Sara flushed; she couldn't help herself. 'I don't know what you're talking about and I don't think you're funny, if that's what you're trying to be,' she said hotly.

'I've never been more serious in my life.'

'Discuss them with Felicia, then; I should think she'd be more suitable.' Sara angrily turned her back on him and walked towards the kitchen. Who the hell was he to think he could worm his way into her apartment? Hadn't he tortured her enough already? Perhaps he was looking for another fling in the hay. Well, he had a surprise coming if he thought she had any intention of . . .

'Sara.' Lee's voice was gentle; the hand on her shoulder surprisingly hard.

'Leave me alone,' she muttered, her face averted so he wouldn't see the angry tears in her eyes. 'Can't you see that I . . . don't want you here?'

'Sara.' He was insistent. 'Is there any chance of your getting pregnant?'

So that was what he was after! Sara thought furiously. Leave it to a man to be worrying about his mythical powers of procreation! 'No.'

'It was your first time, wasn't it?'

She flung off his hand and turned to face him. 'It's none of your damned business,' she said.

'Isn't it?' His eyes were dark and intense under their black brows.

'No. You have no hold over me,' she spat at him. 'I don't belong to you.'

Lee studied the hot blue of her eyes, the flush on her pale cheeks and the tense set of her body. 'Yes, you do,' he said. 'I'm planning to marry you.'

Sara stared at him for one incredulous moment, and then she understood. Lee wasn't convinced that she wouldn't get pregnant from their night together. He'd guessed that it was her first time with a man, knew that she hadn't taken any precautions and was now, in some twisted sense of manly honour, prepared to give her an honest name. 'Surprise,' she said sweetly, 'but I prefer to remain single.'

'Sara, I . . .'

'Marry Felicia if you're so eager to put a ring on someone's finger.'

'Damn it, Sara . . .'

'Or the thousands of other women who would only be too happy, ecstatic in fact,' Sara went on, unable to keep the bitterness from her voice, 'to join with you in honest matrimony. Although I don't know why you bother. After all, your bedroom is a three-ring circus, isn't it? One woman after another, a never-ending . . .'

Lee silenced her the only way he knew how. He pulled her rigid, resistant body into his arms and bent his dark head over hers. Sara felt his lips touch hers and she tried to fight the potent force of his kiss. She didn't want to yield to him; she didn't want him to know just how powerful his attraction was, but she couldn't help the way her mouth parted under his or the way her eyes closed in submission when his hand ran so possessively down her back.

'Now,' he said quietly, lifting his head and staring down into her wide, blue eyes, 'will you promise not to talk for five minutes?'

'I . . .'

He placed a finger on her trembling lips. 'Five minutes,' he said. 'Promise?'

She nodded and Lee, taking her by the hand as if she were a small child, led her back into the living room and pulled her down on the couch beside him.

'I want to marry you,' he said, 'and not because I think you might be pregnant or any of the other crazy reasons you've conjured up in your head. I've known that I wanted to marry you since that day in the Hotel

Moravia. You were the first woman I'd ever met who didn't give a damn who I was; you hated me from the start.'

Sara opened her mouth, but he shook his head, silencing her.

'It was refreshing to be thoroughly disliked after being adored, adulated and worshipped. You're right; I have my pick of women and, frankly, I'd gotten to the point where I couldn't care less. You might find this hard to believe, but when I met you, I hadn't slept with a woman in months and I hadn't met one in years that I liked. And then you walked into the scene; furious, outraged and completely unimpressed by my status. In fact, it was the very thing about me that attracted women that turned you off.' He gave a sudden grin. 'Sara, I fell in love the moment you sat down with your knees so tight together you could have held a pin between them and glared at me as if I were the most repugnant man alive.'

'Oh, Lee,' was all Sara could say. Her voice was husky with happiness; her eyes had softened to a deep blue velvet.

He took her hands in his and turned them over, looking down at her palms as if he could read his future in their lines. 'I did everything in my power to see you without coming on so strong that you'd take flight. But everywhere I turned, the damn play was stuck between us like an obstacle course. I couldn't play the role of Dr Holme any other way than the one I'd envisioned, but I knew how angry it made you.'

'Furious,' she agreed softly.

'I decided to court you in an old-fashioned sense. I'd been so used to women throwing themselves at my head that I didn't know quite how to act. I began with roses, and when that didn't get a response, I bought the charms for you. The minute I saw you in the theatre, I knew you were going to give them back, so I had to be more blunt about being interested in you. Then we had dinner here and ended up fighting over the play again. There were times,' he told her with mock-menace, 'that I would have thoroughly enjoyed wringing your neck!'

'I thought you used the flowers and charms to get me into the theatre. I was convinced that the only reason you were interested in me was to pick my brains for the play.'

He raised her left hand and kissed her palm, making her shiver. 'I always wanted to understand what made you write *Adjustments* the way you did.' She started to speak and he silenced her. 'Wait, my confession's not over. I was more frightened of opening night than I'd been of anything in my life, not only for myself but for you. I knew when you saw the play in its entirety that I'd be back to square one with you. My only chance, at least the way I saw it, was to see you before the opening and convince you that I loved you. Unfortunately,' his mouth twisted wryly, 'it didn't quite work out the way I'd planned. We fought, we argued, and we might have ended up in bed, but nothing was resolved, and the next morning it all fell apart again.'

'I thought you just needed a body to keep you warm that night,' Sara confessed. 'Why didn't you tell me you loved me?'

'I tried, but I couldn't. The more we talked that night, the more I realised that I didn't know how you felt. If I told you that I loved you, I was afraid you'd laugh in my face. Then when you told me that you'd slept with me just for the experience, I ... well, I wanted to kill you.'

She reached up and touched the corner of his mouth with its bitter slant. 'I regretted saying it,' she said softly. 'I knew how much you hated women who tried to use you that way.'

Lee sighed. 'So I took my revenge the way I knew best. Felicia and I are friends; we had a mutual drinking binge one night where we confessed that we were both hopelessly in love with the wrong people and weren't a bit attracted to one another despite the efforts of the publicity people. She was just as surprised at that kiss as you were; you're not the only one who needed an apology. It was a rotten thing to do.'

'It worked, though,' Sara admitted with a grim laugh. 'I've never been more jealous in my life!'

Lee leaned forward and brushed his lips against hers. 'Good,' he murmured. 'I like it when you get jealous.'

Sara leaned her head against his shoulder as he pulled her into the curve of his arm. 'I already hate all those women who hang around you because you're a movie star,' she said.

'There won't be any more.'

Surprised, she glanced up into his face. 'What do you mean?'

'No more movies. I've made more than enough money and I don't like the notoriety. I've discovered that I prefer the stage anyway. It'll make for a quieter life.'

A thought suddenly struck Sara. 'If you were afraid to tell me that you loved me, then why did you come today?' she asked' 'You haven't taken no for an answer yet.'

'Two warriors came to your aid,' said Lee with a laugh.

'Two warriors?'

'One in a long red gown and one in black with granny glasses and an army of cats with biblical names.'

Sara gave a soft laugh. 'Fiona and my Aunt Betty.'

'They met, exchanged notes and ganged up on me,' he groaned. 'They shoved me into a corner and told me that I was a cad, a louse and a heel. Your aunt has a rather ... unique way of expressing herself. As far as she was concerned, I should be honoured that her niece had fallen in love with me, and if I remember correctly, no man west of the Atlantic, east of the Mississippi, south of Canada and north of Mexico had the right to refuse her.'

Sara couldn't help laughing at the thought of Lee at the mercy of her aunt. 'There's no stopping Aunt Betty when she's on the warpath,' she agreed.

'Fiona was a bit more elegant, but not much. She told me that I was a damned fool if I let my pride get the better of me and let you go. She even went so far as to boycott me from her dinner parties if I didn't march myself out of that hotel and go after you. I confess that I had to wait and muster my forces until today. I needed a night to figure out my strategy.'

Sara unbuttoned the neck of his shirt and put her hand on the warm skin of his muscles. 'We both tried to hurt one another,' she said with regret, then looked up at him with teasing eyes. 'May I suggest several weeks of tender, loving care to make up for it?'

Lee's arm tightened around her. 'Mmmm, feels good to me.'

'Sounds good,' she corrected him.

He placed his hand over the one she had inside his shirt. 'No, it feels good,' he said softly, and buried his face in the thick coppery strands of her hair. 'Sara, don't ever stop touching me. I've wanted you for so long.'

Sara slipped her other arm around his waist. 'Oh, Lee,' she sighed, her lips against the warm, strong hollow of his throat. 'We've wasted so much time!'

'Months,' he agreed.

'I never understood until today why I kept pushing my feelings down and out of sight, but I talked with my mother this morning and . . .'

She could feel Lee tense slightly. 'About the psychiatrist?'

Sara nodded. 'I was right, actually. The real Dr Holme never manipulated me the way he does Maria in the play, but ... oh, Lee, it's hard to explain,' she sighed with frustration. 'I hardly understand it myself.'

'I'm listening.'

'I was the one who had sexual feelings, Lee, not the doctor. My mother told me that I had a crush on him; they both knew it, but considered it normal for a young girl to fall in love with her analyst. The trouble was that I felt so guilty about wanting to sleep with him that I forced myself to forget that I'd ever felt that way. Every time I had any sort of sexual yearnings after that, I would suppress them. When you met me, I was living a totally asexual life; you forced me to be aware of my feelings, but I wasn't very thankful. I fought you all along the way.'

'Unmercifully,' he said drily.

'I think that when I wrote the play,' Sara went on, her brow furrowed in concentration, 'I subconsciously made Dr Home sexually manipulative. I couldn't face putting the blame on Maria where it belonged. I was too close to the character; I identified too strongly with her.'

'So you're not angry with me any more,' Lee murmured.

'Of course I am,' she said, pushing herself away from him in mock-indignation. 'You poked and prodded and didn't give me a moment's peace!'

He softly caressed her cheek with his hand. 'I had no choice. I could sense that wall you'd put around yourself and wanted desperately to break it down, but I was never sure that if I pushed you too far you wouldn't be frightened off. During the ride back to your apartment after Fiona's party, I wanted to make love to you in the taxi, but I restrained myself,' he grinned down at her, 'with difficulty.'

'I wanted you to,' she told him. 'You'll never know how much.'

'Yes, I will,' he said, a glint of fire deep in his dark eyes. 'You're going to show me.'

Sara began to complete the job of unbuttoning his shirt. 'When?' she asked, her eyes lowered demurely, their lashes fanning her cheek.

'Witch,' he growled. 'As soon as you admit that you fell in love with me at first sight and will marry me as soon as possible.'

She pulled his shirt out of the waist of his jeans. 'Your ego is already oversized,' she said, her hand stroking the flat planes of his chest, her fingers curling in the triangle of dark hair. 'I remember quite plainly your saying that no woman was worth the sacrifice of your career.'

'I didn't mean you,' he said huskily.

Her hand descended to the taut muscles of his abdomen. 'I'm not sure you deserve this,' she pouted. 'After all, you've been rotten and mean,' her fingers slid beneath the jeans, 'and . . .'

'Sara . . .' gritted Lee, his hand gripping her wrist, his voice caught somewhere between a groan and a threat, 'answer me!'

'I love you,' she said simply, then pulled his head down so their lips met, whispering as she did, 'I always have.'